EGAN CANYON
STATION

A PONY EXPRESS WESTERN ADVENTURE
INSPIRED BY TRUE EVENTS

Russell J. Atwater

Contents

Chapter One
New to Salt Lake City

*T*he *Emerald Isle* wasn't the worst saloon in Salt Lake City, but not far off it. It had been an abandoned feed store before McParland bought the place. No one knew where he got the money or how he kept it going. There were all kinds of rumors and dark speculation from the regulars. McParland himself would joke that it only took three dedicated alcoholics to keep a tavern going. They would drink to his health for that. Tonight was busy, though: four men stared intensely at their cards, playing Faro.

"What can I get you, friend?" McParland asked the young man who stepped in from the street and looked about the bar. The floor was strewn with sawdust and they dotted the room with spittoons. The young man looked like he might leave if McParland hadn't noticed him.

"What you got?" he asked. He was tall and wore dusty work clothes. McParland studied him as he came in and sat at the end of the bar. McParland stood before him, moving aside a few of the rags his customers used to wipe their moustaches clean.

"Beer's a quarter and whiskey's fifty cents."

"Beer, I guess," the young man murmured.

McParland returned with a smudged glass filled with watered down beer.

"That'll be two bits."

He watched the kid fumble around in his pockets for the money. Looked like he wouldn't be staying long.

"You new to town?" McParland asked, taking the coins.

"Yeah," he gave McParland a guarded look.

"Well. Let me give you some advice..."

Before McParland could impart his wisdom, a yell came from the center of the room. One of the poker players was standing, a knife protruding from the palm of his right hand.

"You skunk! You stabbed my hand!" yelled the man. He was short and dressed in a fine cream suit, rapidly staining with blood.

"Well," drawled his attacker, named Pierce. "That hand was cheatin'."

McParland rushed over to the table.

"I've warned you before, Pierce. Are you all right, Mr. Winston? Your hand..."

Brushing the saloon keeper away, Winston drew the bloody knife from his hand. Looking at the weapon, his face turned as pale as his suit.

"Damn you, Pierce!" he cried, lunging forward with the weapon. Pierce fell back from his chair. Pierce was known as a mean drunk. Sober, he was soft-spoken and polite. Once he had taken a drink, and especially when he was losing at poker, he turned nasty and fearful. McParland generally kicked him out before he got too bad. After some cajoling and petitioning, and more charming when sober, he often found his way back into *The Emerald Isle*. Tonight he was holding off a knife from a furious Mr. Winston.

"You don't want to point that thing at me," he said through gritted teeth. The other card players stood back. The truth was, they were afraid of Winston. Unlike Pierce, he was mean all the time. He also ran the brothel next door, which was why he dressed like a dandy. A few of his girls had disappeared down through the years and nobody asked too many questions.

"I'll point it right through your eye," Winston said. His own eyes were wide with a cruel gleam, his good hand forcing the blade closer to Pierce's face. The bitter smile on his face belied the blood oozing out of his left palm. Pierce was sobering rapidly as the urgency of his situation impressed itself.

"Listen, Winston. I didn't mean nothin' by it. I'll...I'll get yer hand fixed up. Ain't nobody here going to help me?"

Most people at the saloon that night knew Winston and Pierce, so they figured the result was inevitable. Pierce had had it coming for a long time and Winston...Well, who was going to mess with someone like that? It would take someone pretty foolhardy.

Winston yelped in shock as the knife was kicked out of his hand. Both he and Pierce stared in surprise at the young stranger.

"You don't need to kill him, Mister," said the young man.

Winston's eyelids flickered, eyes rolling back as he slumped forward onto Pierce. He fainted as the blood loss caught up with his cold rage. Pierce wriggled underneath the dead weight of the man.

"Hey!" he cried. "He's bleedin' on me."

The door swung open. McParland had sized up the situation early and decided his best option was to get the law. The sheriff's station was half a mile away, but they knew his deputy frequented the brothel. Winston's brothel. The deputy's trousers looked hastily pulled on.

"Mr. Winston," the deputy exclaimed, as he ran forward to straighten him up. The others found this a good point to get involved. Soon, they had a pale and bleary Winston perched in a chair.

"You!" the deputy yelled at Pierce, sidling towards the door. He pulled his gun, pointing at the man. "Move and yer a goner!"

"I ain't done nothin'," Pierce said, raising his hands. "I was just playin' cards."

"You're under arrest," the deputy said. "For the assault on Mr. Winston here. Somebody bandage his hand or it'll be a murder."

"Anyone got bandages?" asked one of the card players. There was confusion as everyone spoke at once. During the noise, the young stranger reached down and picked up the bloody knife. Everyone went silent as he used it to rip a strip from Winston's suit. He wrapped it tight around the wounded palm. Winston came to and regarded him, calculating.

"Why, you're a regular hero, ain't you?" he said. "What's your name, son?"

"Stone. Mitchell Stone."

"I'll remember that name."

The look he gave Mitchell was terrifying. McParland took charge.

"Deputy. I want every charge you can think of laid against Pierce here. Boys. How about you take Mr. Winston home? You know where to go."

The others scrambled to aid the wounded man. Winston went weak again and allowed himself to lean on their shoulders as they led him next door. They were tripping over each other to assist him, in the hopes of some free hospitality at Winston's establishment. The deputy kept his gun trained on Pierce's back. Pierce looked back at Mitchell, giving him a genial smile.

"Thank you, Mitchell. I reckon I owe you one."

"Git outa here," McParland growled. "I never want to see you in here again. You've upset my customers for the last time."

"Wasn't me," Pierce said, smiling peacefully. "It was that terrible whiskey you serve."

"Come on," the Deputy said. "I got some fine spirits for you back at the station."

Pierce shook his head ruefully, allowing himself to be led away. McParland looked at the mess of his saloon with a sigh: upended chairs, broken glass, and spilt liquor.

"Going to be a long night," he muttered.

"Say," asked Mitchell. "What was the advice you were going to give me?"

McParland looked him up and then chuckled and said.

"Don't get involved in other folk's business. You'll regret it."

***

Mitchell nursed his drink while the saloon owner busied about. Even when watered down, there was a foul edge to the beer's bitterness. Mitchell had little experience with drinking since he lit out from home back in Wichita. His parents had been strict Methodists and didn't indulge. He was making a point these days of doing everything his folks never let him do. He took another swallow of his beer. It wasn't so bad after a while. He looked into the nearly empty glass and thought about his nearly empty pockets. What would he do next?

"They say McParland's cat gets into the beer sometimes. That's the special flavor."

Mitchell looked up. A rangy middle-aged man was smirking down at him. He was dressed lightly: a bright red bandana around his neck, a skullcap over his sandy hair.

"Mind if I join you?"

Mitchell shook his head, looking back down.

"Name's Donald Russell. Call me Don."

As he sat, the spurs of his boots made a metallic clanking sound. In all the commotion, Mitchell hadn't noticed him before.

"You some kind of jockey, Mister?" Mitchell said. "You're sure dressed like one."

Don smiled, leaning back.

"You could say that. Know how to race horses?"

"Me? Naw. Only ever rode farm horses. My Pa would give us a hidin' if we ran 'em too fast."

Don nodded, lost in thought.

"McParland," he called out after a minute. "Bring over two whiskeys. Least you could do after this man broke up that fight. The good bottle too, mind. Not that coffin varnish you usually serve."

McParland stopped sweeping around the card table. He looked like he was going to argue, but thought better of it. He grunted and departed to get a bottle. Mitchell noticed the shining Colt strapped to Don's leg.

"You don't mind, do you?" Don asked. "Least I can do. By rights, McParland should put it on the house. He's as tight a skinflint as you'll meet. Plus, he's trying to figure out if Mr. Winston will take against you or not."

"Oh? I don't care."

"Hmm. You might. Winston's got a cruel side. There are stories."

McParland bustled over with two glasses.

"Thank you kindly," Don said.

"That'll be…" he looked at Don, then forced a smile. "On the house."

"Why that's mighty generous. Although, some might say you ought to give the entire bottle to this young man."

"Don't got any money to spare," McParland groused, returning to his sweeping.

"You got him to give us free whiskey?" Mitchell whispered, eyes round with amazement.

"Well," Don said. "I've been coming here on and off for several years. Ain't the first time there's been a ruckus in here. I reckon old McParland owes me a favor or two. What about you? What made you get involved? Pierce, that good-for-nothing whose skin you saved, he's been asking for it for years. Some men, they can't help it. But you? Why'd you stick your neck out?"

"Dunno," Mitchell said. "Ma and Pa were always fightin' at home. I hated it. When I got big enough, I told 'em both to quit or I'd…"

Mitchell took a drink from his glass. He winced as the hot fire of the drink hit his belly.

"Ugh!" he coughed, shaking his head. "That's worse than beer."

Don Russell's laughter at Mitchell's expense was not unkind.

"You'll get used to it. Don't swig it so. Where you from, Mitchell Stone?"

"How'd you know my name?"

"I watched the whole show earlier, remember? Judging by your accent, you sound like you're from back East."

"Kansas," Mitchell said. "I grew up on a farm outside Witchita."

"How'd you make it all the way out to Salt Lake?"

"Hitched a ride on a cattle train. Got me to Denver. I done some herding in the mountains. It don't pay so well. Thought I'd keep heading west."

Don nodded, taking a large swig of whiskey.

"And what's next?"

Mitchell looked down, a defeated look on his face.

"Truth is, I'm broke. Thought I'd ask around for work come morning. I shouldn't have spent my last on beer, but I was so fed up."

Don clapped him on the back.

"Hey now! Turns out this is your lucky day. I saw the way you broke up that fight without thinking twice. That's a true sign of character! I'm always on the lookout for promising young men like yourself. 'Specially these days."

"You are?" Mitchell asked. "It ain't illegal, is it?"

"Absolutely not! On the contrary, we're as near to the law in some places we breeze through. Look. You thought maybe I was a jockey? I'm a Pony Express rider. Well, I guess you could say I'm a half-rider. The company has me down as Hiring Manager these days. Although I have hit the trail occasionally. We're always short good men. Just back from Sacramento, in fact."

"Oh, what's the pay?"

"Good man! Figuring out the angles. We have a couple of weeks probation. Once you're in, it'll be one hundred and twenty five a month."

Mitchell's mouth hung open at the vast sum.

"Yep," Don said. "It's good money. Not everyone makes it through probation, though. Got some training for you to do, seein' as how yer not a racer. Mr. Alexander Majors, one of the founders, he believes in paying top dollar to get the best men."

"Pro... Probation? Ain't that like what a saint has to do? Starvation and such."

Mitchell recalled the preacher thundering about some saint fasting and suffering privation in the desert.

"What? No, no. Jus' means you don't get paid until we see you can handle the job. Speakin' of which, you got a sweetheart? I bet a handsome feller like you has one in every town."

Don asked lightly, studying Mitchell's reaction intensely.

"Well. I guess Isabelle back home said she'd wait for me. I don't rightly know though..."

"You married?" Don barked the question, causing Mitchell to start.

"Ah, no. It ain't like that. She's awful pretty, an' all. Her Pa owns the store in town, so..."

"Good. Mr. Majors insists on bachelors. You'll forget about her once you get ridin'. Money like this means you can save it up. Return to that sweetheart with a nice parcel. If you've a mind to..."

"What about you, Mister Russell? You savin' for someone?"

"Me?" Don snorted. "First, don't call me Mister. Don's fine. Pony express rider's always movin'. I don't got much time for settlin' down. Sometimes, when you take a bit of vacation, you can visit someplace like Winston's next door. Don't have the time for it, though. One other question. How old are you?"

"Uh, eighteen," Mitchell lied.

Don nodded.

"Good answer. So. What if I were to offer you to join the Pony Express?"

Mitchell looked at the rangy man sitting across from him. The money was more than he could imagine right now, but something about the eager light in Don's eye gave him pause. Of course, he had heard of the Pony express. One wrangler he travelled down from Colorado with had pointed out a distant dot racing across the horizon to him.

"That's an express rider," his companion said. "They sleep on the backs of their horses."

Don sensed Mitchell's unease, drank back his whiskey and grimaced.

"Well. How about it?"

"It's an awful generous offer, Don. I'd like to sleep on it, if you don't mind."

"Sure. Not like I expect you to sign up tonight, anyway. Where were you fixin' to hang yer hat tonight?"

"I dunno. Thought maybe I'd ask the saloon keep if he had a room. Maybe help around the place tomorrow to pay for it."

"McParland?" Don called out without looking away from Mitchell. "You got any room here?"

McParland ambled over to their table.

"Maybe. Who's asking?"

"My young friend here. I'll cover however much you were going to charge for that flea-infested bunk you got out back."

"That's mighty kind of you, Mister. I mean Don. How can I repay you?"

"Never mind. Instead of moping around here tomorrow, you got to promise to come down to the Pony Express station first thing. Now, finish up that whiskey 'fore I change my mind."

Mitchell complied, swallowing back the last of his glass. His eyes watered as the liquor set his throat alight. It wasn't as bad this time around. Don stood, stretching his long lanky body. He stuck out a hand in Mitchell's direction. Mitchell quickly rose to shake it.

"Well then," said Don. "Reckon I'll head next door. Been on the trail too long. Need to limber up a little."

He reached into his pocket and produced a dollar for McParland.

"That oughta cover it," he said. "See ya tomorrow."

McParland, holding onto his broom, watched Russell depart.

"Well," he said. "You sure impressed old Russell with all that fightin'. You thinkin' of joining his band of yahoos?"

"I ain't sure," Mitchell said. "What're they like?"

"They're all a bit like him, I s'pose. They got plenty of money to splash around. You'd think they were greased lightnin' the way they talk. You gotta be fast, I reckon. Travel through lawless territory like that. Comanche, Paiute, all them tribes don't take kindly to men galloping through at all hours, in all kinds of weather."

Mitchell smiled.

"I suppose I'll check out his outfit tomorrow."

"You do that. All right, Mister Pony Express. Your bunk's this way."

Mitchell followed the barman to a door behind the bar.

"You got a bag?" McParland said, from the other side of the door.

"Nope," said Mitchell. "I travel light."

McParland shook his head.

"Follow me then. It ain't fancy, mind. You go next door for that. Very good value considerin' what you paid."

The lodgings at *The Emerald Isle* were sparse, but Mitchell didn't mind over much. McParland ushered him into a narrow room with a bow-backed cot. It was obvious McParland didn't get too many sleeping customers, as they had to clear out a couple of casks of beer before Mitchell could settle himself down.

Head swimming from beer, whiskey, and the excitement of the night's events, it took Mitchell a while to calm down enough to start to slumber. Half asleep, a noise like an axed pine tree cracking jolted him awake. He jerked up, looking around in the darkness for the danger. In his confused state, he couldn't remember where he was or how he got there.

After a brief silence, a low growl begun. It sounded at first like a beast threatening another. Recollecting himself, it dawned on Mitchell that McParland had said his own room was next to this one and he was snoring. Mitchell couldn't believe a healthy man could make such a terrible noise. It was a long night. Throughout the small hours, Mitchell listened as the rumble built and built, culminating in a snarl that sounded like it would be the man's last breath.

***

Dust motes danced around the shaft of sunlight that had broken into Mitchell's dank room. It took a long while for the light to reach where he slept. He had been sleeping outdoors for weeks and even this mean narrow cot was a welcome reprieve. Because of the ruckus on the other side of the wall, it took another long while for the light to bring him awake. Mitchell groaned, remembering the night before: the fight and the whiskey and the… He sat bolt upright. The job!

He pulled on his clothes. *First thing I'm going to buy is new clothes*, he thought as he hastily made for the door. Out in the saloon, McParland was nowhere to be found. Instead, Winston was sitting at the table alongside a woman in a white dress. She was playing solitaire and sipping tea from a chipped china cup. She had thick wavy hair and piercing green eyes. Mitchell did a double take at Winston. His face was a shade paler than most normal people. Aside from that and a clean bandaged hand, he looked exactly the same as last night. Mitchell wondered at his clean white suit. There was no way he could have got all that blood out.

"Esmeralda," said Winston. "This is Mitchell Stone."

The woman in white inclined her head, coquettishly batting false eyelashes.

"You never said he was so good-looking."

Mitchell gulped. She reminded him of the illustration of a queen from one of his school books.

"Um. Thank you, Ma'am. I... I should get going. I've gotta...."

"Sit!" Winston barked. He straightened his shoulders, calming himself. "McParland told me all about Russell offering you a spot with the Pony Express. I've a better offer for you."

Mitchell considered his options. Why was he so sure he wanted to join Don?

"All right," he said, sitting across from the pair.

"Seems to me like you're good in a fight," said Winston. "You might even say I owe you."

He raised his bandaged hand.

"I don't like owing people," he continued. "It's a weakness. In return, I'm willing to give you a chance. Make something of yourself as my man."

"Mr. Winston's had men before, but none as fine as you," gushed Esmeralda. "Remember Stan. He was a stinking brute."

She wrinkled her nose, pouting her painted lips.

"It's too bad how he—"

"Shut up, Es." Winston said with a thin grin. "Never mind about Stan. I need someone else to keep off the likes of that rat last night. I know the deputy. I'm thinking we get him to release Pierce and we have a bit of fun with him." He raised his bandaged hand. "Looks like he'll leave me a scar. I owe him at least one in return. Maybe a few more as interest. Like I said, I don't like owing people."

Mitchell felt an icy shiver at the calm cruelty of Winston's words.

"I'll set you up nice. *The Golden Lily* is my establishment next door. I got rooms and all kinds of sportin' women. Esmeralda here's my hiring manager. Although she's not above doing whatever business I need doing."

Mitchell noticed a momentary look of dread on Esmeralda's face before she hid it with a glittering laugh.

"Why, Mr. Winston! I believe a hero like Mitchell here will have my girls falling over themselves for his… affections."

"I insist he pay," Winston said, banging the table for emphasis. "Everyone pays. Nothing or no one's free. You do the job right, you'll have more money than that Pony Express manager ever could hand out. Now, whad'ya say?"

Winston's smile was as enticing as a rattlesnake's. Mitchell looked at Esmeralda, who gave him a narrow shake of her head.

"Thanks for helpin' me decide," Mitchell said. "Reckon I'll head out."

He stood and went for the door.

"You come back here," Winston called, voice shrill. "No one in Salt Lake City walks away from me! You know why Don Russell's scrounging about dives like this one, looking for drifters to run his ponies? Most of 'em don't make it past the first week. Some fall off their horses in the night, dashed to bits at the bottom of some canyon. Those are the lucky ones. Others get robbed by bandits or scalped by Indians. You really want to risk all that compared to what I'm offering you? Hey! You answer me."

Mitchell had paused by the door to listen to the man's ranting. He turned back to see the gun, a pearl-handled derringer. Winston had slipped it from his pocket, training the snub double barrel on Mitchell. With a shock, Mitchell realized the man had planned to shoot him in the back. Esmeralda gave him an indecipherable look before elbowing her teacup onto Winston. His attention on Mitchell, Winston didn't notice her deliberate action.

"Oh, Mr. Winston!" she exclaimed. "I'm truly sorry."

Winston started at the spill. As he cursed his companion, the little pistol went off. The gun was in his left hand, not his shooting hand. The bullet smashed into a mirror over the bar, destroying the only decoration of any worth in The Emerald Isle. Mitchell dashed out the door. His last view was of Esmeralda making a fuss over a furious Winston. Distracting her employer by cajoling and dabbing at his fine suit, Mitchell realized she had saved his life.

***

Mitchell rushed out onto the busy street. The noon sun beat down as he ran past horses and clattering wagons. A herd of longhorn cattle bellowed and moaned, unused to all the people and buildings. A pair of men yelled and whipped at them. Mitchell paused, bending over and panting. He looked back. No sign of Winston.

"You alright, mister?"

A barefoot urchin with a torn shirt squinted up at Mitchell.

"Hey, kid," Mitchell said, catching his breath. "Gimme a minute."

The kid shrugged. He was sitting on the steps outside a boarding house.

"Pony Express?" Mitchell recovered enough to ask. "Know where the Pony Express station is?"

"Maybe. I'm awful hungry though. Can't recollect properly."

Mitchell scrutinized the child, wondering if everyone in this town was on the make.

"Listen, kid. I got nothin'. Just tell me what direction it's at. I'm in a hurry."

The child considered.

"People nowadays got no Christian charity, y'know," he sighed. "Anyway. You go down this street, turn left at the bank. The Express station is past there. The old federal livery. Once part of the garrison. I've heard–"

"Thanks!"

Mitchell cut off the rambling account and took off at speed. The child shook his head and clicked his tongue, watching him go. Mitchell made it to the old stables as fast as he could. Instead of a proper sign outside, there was a large poster pasted on a wooden signboard. Mitchell paused to read it, catching his breath before making his way in.

PONY EXPRESS!

———————

10 Days New York to San Francisco!
CHANGE OF TIME!
REDUCED RATES!

...

Mitchell realized he was sweating heavily as he studied the rates and engraving of a rider on a horse. The pony looked to be in flight, all feet well off the ground. He had a bugle to his mouth with a banner that said "NEWS!" flowing out of it. A fit of nervousness overcame Mitchell. Was this really what he wanted? He realized that running away from things had become something of a habit. Why stop now? He stared again at the engraving of the pony in flight. Why, he thought, let's keep running, but get paid for it.

He took a deep breath and walked through the open gates into the yard. They corralled a few ponies on one side of the yard, tails swishing as they drank from a trough. There was nobody in sight.

"Hullo?" Mitchell called.

No one answered. One pony popped its head up, ears twitching. Mitchell frowned and walked across the yard. A door had a sign with the word "Dispatch" on it. The window alongside it was so dirty it was opaque. Mitchell opened the door. Inside, the room was cool. A hall led down to what looked like rooms for the riders. There was a rollback desk against one wall, strewn with many dockets and receipts. Don Russell sat in a chair, his back to Mitchell. He was writing into a ledger book, a quill and ink well to his right. Another man, about Mitchell's age, was lying on his back on a bench. He appeared to be asleep, his face covered by his hat.

Mitchell cleared his throat.

"Don. Ah. Mr. Russell. Sorry I'm late. I..."

Don turned and looked up, chair creaking. He frowned at Mitchell. The spectacles he wore made him look older.

"Well, look who it is..."

His avuncular manner had changed from the night before.

"I... I know you said come first thing," Mitchell said. "I had a terrible night of it. Then Mr. Winston came by and–"

"Do you know what it means to be late in the Pony Express?" Don's words were quiet, anger just beneath the surface. "It means you're out. After I gave you such a generous advance as a night at *The Emerald Isle*. You got some sand, son. Comin' in here this late."

Mitchell swallowed, his fresh hopes dashed.

"I'm real sorry I let you down, Mr. Russell. I want to join. I really do. I shoulda just left with you last night."

"Real sorry, are you?" Don asked. "Well, that ain't good enough. You best get out of here before you wake Frank over there." He nodded towards the young man lying on the bench. "He's not long in from Hanging Rock *and* he was an hour early. Go on. Git!"

Mitchell nodded, ears burning with shame. He turned back towards the door, mind racing at what to do next. Probably he'd have to leave town. A snake like Winston probably would have the word out about him.

Don and Frank exploded with laughter. Frank had to sit up, he was laughing so hard.

"Go on. Git!" he mimicked.

Mitchell beamed back at him.

"Not bad, eh?" he said, taking off his spectacles to wipe them. "Get back in here, Mitchell. We have a tradition in the Pony Express. You always try an' catch out your fellows. Passes the time and keeps us on our toes. Truth is, I'm only back an hour myself. Had a late night at *The Gold Lily* myself."

Mitchell stared at them, slack-jawed.

"You? You don't mind..." he said.

"Well, don't make a habit of it. This varmint here's Frank. He really made it an hour early."

Frank had an open genial face. He nodded to Mitchell.

"Howdy," he said. "What was that you were saying about Winston? I don't like that skunk myself, in his fancy white duds."

"I... He shot at me."

"That so?" asked Don, sitting up straight. "Nice repayment after you broke up that fight. I guess he didn't like you making him look weak. He was asking me about you last night, after they patched him up. Why'd he try to plug you?"

"He wanted me to work for him," Mitchell said. "As a bodyguard. I didn't like the idea."

"Told you this boy had sand, didn't I?" Don said to Frank. "You stick with us and you don't need to trouble yourself with him. Maybe stay away from *The Gold Lily* for a spell though..."

Mitchell looked from Frank to Don.

"So..." he asked. "Does this mean..."

"It means you're in the Pony Express," Don said, standing up and extending his hand.

Relief flooded Mitchell.

He grinned as he shook Don's hand.

Chapter Two
Welcome to the
Pony Express

The morning was cool and fresh. From the quiet of the Pony Express yard, Mitchell grinned up at the blue sky. Spring was always his favorite time of year: the promise of summer's heat mingled with winter's lingering chill. Back home, he snuck outside whenever he could: skipping school or fleeing his arguing parents. When he finally quit home, it felt like he was just playing extended hooky. But he wasn't glad to have left everything back home. Like a sudden spring shower spoiling everything, his mind strayed to Isabelle, the girl he had left behind.

"Ain't you the early bird," Don exclaimed, emerging into the yard from the office door.

"Good mornin', Don," Mitchell said. "Frank woke me when he left before dawn. I guess I want to get started myself. When do you want me to ride out?"

"Oh, ho," Don said with a chuckle. "I let you out there now and you'll be a goner before the day is out. Besides, we have paperwork and such to wrangle with. Come back in here an' we'll have ourselves some breakfast."

Mitchell turned and followed him into the office, noticing for the first time that Don was only wearing a tattered union suit.

"Got to use the privy first," muttered Don, scratching his chest. "Mess is through that way."

Mitchell looked toward Don's nod, past the bunks to a room at the end of the hall.

"You head down there. Cook should be up by now."

Mitchell walked down the long hall to the dark room. His stomach rumbled as he picked up the smell of cooking. Inside were a couple of tables with a large cast-iron range along the back wall. A tiny high window faced onto the street outside, providing the only light. In the gloom, a stooped, white-haired man was pouring batter from a can to make griddle cakes. A large enamel coffee pot gurgled alongside him.

Mitchell cleared his throat, not wanting to surprise the cook. He got no response as the old man busied away at the range. Mitchell shrugged and sat down, looking longingly at the food. Several shelves lined the walls, filled with cups, plates and provisions. A stack of already-cooked griddle cakes sat steaming on the counter. There was another plate of already cooling strips of sowbelly. Mitchell coughed again, impatience and hunger getting the better of him. No response.

"Excuse me," he said. "Wonderin' if I can get some breakfast."

The cook made no response. He just kept humming tunelessly to himself, turning the griddle cakes with his spatula. Mitchell wondered what would happen if he went up and helped himself. He recalled the impulsive way he had interfered in the fight between Winston and Pierce. Wasn't that what his folks were always yelling about? His being too impulsive. Once, his old man had beaten him for picking an apple off the kitchen table without asking. Beat him hard, too. Mitchell ground his teeth at the memory. He stayed put, watching the old-timer cook away.

"You fastin'?" Don asked, walking in. He was fully dressed now, his tight skull cap back on his head. Don grabbed a plate, piling it with the hotcakes and bacon. He pulled a chipped cup from a shelf and filled it with black coffee.

"I didn't know if I should," Mitchell said, as Don sat down beside him. "The cook…"

"Old Watkins?" Don mumbled between bites. "He's deaf as a post. Don't even know yer here. When the company acquired the place from the army, he was part of the deal. He might not even have noticed everything changed."

Mitchell didn't need to hear any more, jumping up and helping himself to the food. He thought he saw a smirk on the side of the old cook's mouth as he filled a big mug of coffee. He sat down and started eating.

"I was startin' to wonder if it was another of them pranks," Mitchell said, after devouring a couple of cakes.

Don was leaning back in his chair, sipping his coffee.

"No, no. Time to get serious," he said. "Once you got that in yer belly, I'll take you around the station. Show you the ropes. Or some of 'em, anyway. We got to get you to sign a contract too; and take the oath."

Mitchell stopped chewing on the leathery sowbelly.

"Oath?" he mumbled.

"Yep. Ya gotta memorize it too. Company insists on it. Why you gone all pale, son?"

"Sorry," Mitchell said. "I ain't too good at memorizin.'"

"Can't ya read? Lots of cowboys can't. No shame in it. You can still learn the thing off, though. It's only a few lines."

"I can read. I just... When it comes to sittin' still and learnin' something. Well, it's too much. Always hated it in school."

"Why, don't you worry. I'll get Frank or someone to help you out. You don't got to say the oath until probation's up, anyway. Lots of time to fix it in your mind. Also, you gotta learn the names of all the stations on the Pony Express route. In the right order."

Mitchell's expression became even more stricken.

"How many stations?" he asked, voice faint.

"One hundred and ninety," Don announced, voice proud. He chewed on his lower lip as he observed the color drain from the young man's face.

"In the right order? I dunno, Don. Between that and the oath... Maybe I'm not cut out for this..."

Don couldn't keep a straight face any longer and erupted laughing.

"Ha hah! Gotcha again. You really gotta learn to keep a poker face. No need to learn off the stations. But you have to recite the oath. Part of it's about not gamblin' and such. Company don't take too kindly to that. Maybe that's why we got to find other ways of entertaining ourselves."

Mitchell shook his head.

"Dang! You had me there, Don. Thought you said we were bein' serious. Are there really that many stations?"

"Sure are. Some of them ain't much. We call 'em 'swing stations'. You just stop for a few minutes and grab yourself a fresh mount. No mail to pick off or drop off. Swing stations are on the long quiet stretches. Others, like this one here, are what we call 'home stations'. You got bunks and fine *kwee-zeen* to dine on. Like what old Watkins here slaps together. Home stations are where the mail is dispatched from. Stand up there, son."

Mitchell did as he was asked. Don appraised him.

"Jus' checkin'. Good thing yer skinny. I thought you were when I first laid eyes on you. Don't be puttin' on too much weight, now. Easy on them griddle cakes! Going to get you new duds too. That cowboy gear you're wearing'll only slow you down."

"What d'ya mean?"

"It's all about weight. The lighter the load, faster you'll go. Why, I don't even wear a hat, just this light little thing." Don pointed to the skull cap he was wearing. "Some riders wear moccasins instead of boots. I know one character who went about in his long johns. Anyway, we'll get you kitted out proper. What did you say that skunk Winston pulled on you?"

"His gun? I think it was a derringer. Like what... Isabelle's Pa had."

Don let the mention of Mitchell's sweetheart's storekeeper father pass without mention.

"That little pea shooter," he scoffed. "Some riders carry 'em, but most don't even travel with a weapon."

"To keep the weight down." Mitchell said.

"You got it. When the service started first, everyone was carryin' all kinds of firearms for protection. But it cost the company too much in weight. The trick to being in the Pony Express is speed. You gotta be able to outrun the bullets any bandit fires at you. You stop and shoot back, you've already lost."

"How's that, Don?"

"Because stoppin' means you'll miss your delivery. And that's the one thing we don't want. Don't worry, we'll give you one of the lighter Colts we got for your first few runs. Jus' for protection. You'll see, like most, you'll ditch the thing once you get used to the trail."

A couple of other riders came in and saluted Don. Watkins noticed their entry, coughed, and scooped the last of the food he had prepared off the stove. Without a word, he dropped the full plate on the table between the men and shuffled out of the kitchen. The newcomers settled into eating with no further ado.

"Looks like the kitchen's closed," Don said, as he stood up and stretched himself. "Let's get you out to the office and sorted out."

They passed more riders coming in for breakfast as they headed back to the office. Mitchell noticed they were dressed lightly and somewhat on the short side.

"Fellas," Don said, greeting the men. "Come by in a bit after I've got this new fellow sorted out. I've got dispatch orders for you."

"I'd introduce you," Don said as the others hurried past. "But those men are hungry and will be on the road soon after. You'll meet them soon enough."

"That's fine," said Mitchell. "Seems like everythin's done quickly as possible around here."

Don didn't answer as he fished about in his rollback desk for a form.

"Here you go," he said, producing a large piece of paper with "The Pony Express" prominently on the letterhead. "You just sign this, and we can get started."

"I thought I was going on, whad'ya call it... probation."

"Y'are," said Don, scanning the document. "Contract states, 'The Rider must undergo a trial period of two weeks or until it satisfies the hiring manager he is suitable and his conduct is becoming...' and so on and so forth."

Don searched about some more, coming up with an old quill and an inkwell. He looked up at Mitchell.

"Sure you want to do this? Last chance."

Mitchell took a deep breath, then nodded.

"All right," said Don. "I'll get you to sign here."

Mitchell paused over the dotted line, savoring the moment, then scrawled his name onto the contract.

"Good," Don said, adapting a formal tone. "On behalf of our founders, William Russell, Alexander Majors, and William B. Waddell, I welcome you, Mitchell Stone, as a rider for the Pony Express. You will start with a salary of $125 a month, starting after a two-week probation period."

Don held out his hand and Mitchell shook it.

"All right," Don continued. "First thing's first. Your bible."

"Bible?"

"Yep. Every rider's gotta carry one."

Don reached into a wooden crate full of shiny leather-bound volumes. He handed one to Mitchell. It had "Holy

Bible" stamped in gilt on the spine. The cover had the three founders' names in similar lettering. Mitchell stared at it. It was on the large side, even for the word of the Lord.

"I thought we traveled light."

"Mr. Majors is a very Christian man. He feels that the blessings and guidance of the good book offset the physical weight of the volume."

Mitchell raised an eyebrow.

"Rules are rules, I suppose," he said, taking the bible from Don.

"That's right," agreed Don, handing Mitchell a slip of printed paper. "There's the oath. With your hand on the bible, read that out."

Mitchell did as instructed, although he needed help from Don parsing some longer words.

I, _____ , do hereby swear, before the Great and Living God, that during my engagement, and while I am an employee of Russell, Majors, and Waddell, I will, under no circumstances, use profane language, that I will drink no intoxicating liquors, that I will not quarrel or fight with any other employee of the firm, and that in every respect I will conduct myself honestly, be faithful to my duties, and so direct all my acts as to win the confidence of my employers, so help me God.

Mitchell wondered at some restrictions. Hadn't Don met him in a saloon and introduced him to whiskey?

"Well done. Like I said, you got to learn that off for when you come off probation. Just practice it before bed every night."

"I'll try, Don." Mitchell sounded dubious.

"I know all these rules and such sound strict and starched at first. You'll get accustomed to it. Think of the money you'll be earnin' and all the fine countryside you'll be visitin'!"

Mitchell gave Don a thin smile and nodded.

"Right then," Don said, heading for the door. "Let's head over to the Stores an' get the rest of yer kit."

***

The Stores was a long wooden building along the station's outside wall. Across the street, the formidable federal garrison glared down at them. Don noticed Mitchell looking over at the high wall.

"Garrison sold the firm this livery when the operation started. They built a new one on the far side. One thing you'll learn is this company's awful generous with money."

"Are they makin' much in return?" asked Mitchell.

"Who knows? All's I know is they keep paying me. Hold on."

He fished about in his pockets for an iron key, using it to open a heavy padlock.

"C'mon in," he beckoned, ducking his head as he disappeared into the interior. Following him inside, Mitchell blinked twice, his eyes unaccustomed to the warm dimness. He scanned the treasures within while Don disappeared, muttering about Mitchell's likely size. They stacked shelves with sacks of flour, cans, bedding, and all manner of equine equipment.

"Try these for size," Don said as he reappeared, producing a light shirt, pants, and boots. He had a tight knit skullcap perched on top of the bundle, similar to his own.

"I'll spare yer blushes while you change," Don said, smirking. "Best get you a saddle."

Mitchell shrugged and started stripping as Don disappeared again. The clothes were a little loose, but they were new. The leather boots were unusually supple and lightweight. He gladly exchanged them for his own heavy pair.

Don eventually returned with a thin, light looking saddle.

"Good," he said, satisfied Mitchell had changed so quickly. "I'll take them old duds. Looks like they ain't even good enough to give to the church. Maybe we'll burn 'em. You take this."

In exchange for the clothes, he handed the saddle to Mitchell. Mitchell noticed the saddle had a tan leather covering with four pouches, one on each corner.

"That's called a *mochila*," Don explained. "Them pouches are called *cantinas*. That's where the mail goes. I reckon some Spaniard came up with the whole thing. The *Mochila* is your most important possession. Lose yer gun, even the bible, but don't lose this. Or more importantly, what it contains. The *mail*."

There was a gleam in Don's eye as he emphasized the word. Mitchell nodded vigorously, eager to appear agreeable. Secretly, he was surprised by this sudden display of zeal from the mostly laconic manager.

"You study that while I get your hardware."

Hardware? wondered Mitchell as he felt around the pouches. The leather was clean and smelled faintly of saddle soap. He had a sudden image of himself astride a horse, galloping at top speed to deliver whatever precious cargo they secreted here.

Don returned with a long brass trumpet, a belt and holster.

"This here's yer bugle. Wear it slung around yer neck. You gotta blow on that hard as you come up to the swing station. An' blow it three times. That's the proper signal. That way they know to get a mount ready for you. Remember, it's all about speed. Go on. Try it."

Mitchell blew a tentative raspberry into the horn.

"Sounds like a cat farting," snorted Don. "Gimme that."

He took back the instrument, casually handing Mitchell the belt. Shocked, Mitchell realized from the weight that there was a gun in the holster.

"Now you do this…"

He took a deep breath and pursed his lips, the tip of his tongue protruding. His cheeks bellowed out as he blew hard. Mitchell nearly dropped the pistol as a single brassy note rang out in the Stores.

"Ha hah!" Don cackled. "That's how you do it. You can practice that later. Maybe not in the bunk before bed, though. Careful with that now!" He put down the bugle and took back the belt and holster, removing a short-barreled Colt. He held it up, looking down the barrel.

"You keep this well oiled. This one's shorter than the average Colt. They call it the 'Sheriff's Special'. Like I said before, when we started first, fellas were issued two standard Colts *and* a Henry rifle. Well, that just weighed them down. Now, we only issue these."

He handed the gun to Mitchell.

"You much of a shot?" said Don.

"Mostly crows with my Pa's rifle."

Don made a clicking sound with his tongue.

"You got a lot of things to practice, don't ya? We'll make a regular one-man circus out of you: recitin' oaths, blowin' bugles, and firin' pistols into the air!"

Mitchell smiled. He liked the heft of the pistol in his hand. He turned the chamber experimentally.

"No bullets," he said.

"I'll get you a box later." Don said. "There's one other thing we got to sort out. And that's ridin'. Grab all that gear and foller me over to the corral."

Mitchell did as instructed, accompanying Don over to the enclosure.

"You can pitch it down there," Don said, indicating an untidy livery rack beside the gate. "These are all fine ponies. The company is very particular about that. Go on in. Get used to 'em. I got to attend to the boys waitin' on deliveries."

Don took off in a hurry towards the office. Mitchell spotted two riders standing by the door, smoking rolled cigarettes. With a shrug, Mitchell dropped his new equipment by the gate to the corral. He unlatched the fence and walked in. The horses were indeed fine. One big sorrel came over and nudged at Mitchell with his nose. Stroking the animal's smooth flank, Mitchell marveled again at how no expense seemed to be spared for the Pony Express.

"Hello there," he said to the pony. "Looks like you and me have ended up at a good spot."

"No harm in talkin' to your horse," came a voice from behind Mitchell. "Just don't get too attached."

Mitchell turned in mild surprise. The speaker was carrying his saddle against his chest, its *mochila* laden with mail. He wore light clothes similar to Mitchell's, and out of one corner of his mouth dangled a cigarette.

"Sorry," said Mitchell. "Don said to get acquainted with the animals."

The man nodded as he expertly placed the saddle on the back of the sorrel Mitchell had been petting. Quick as anything, he had it hitched and secured.

"S'fine. First one gets a saddle over, gets to call the pony theirs for the day. Like I said, no point in gettin' too attached. Name's Jonah. Grab me a harness, would ya?"

Jonah nodded towards the rack of bridles and harnesses by the gate. Mitchell grabbed a harness, strapping it on to the patient animal. Jonah took a deep pull on his smoke, then spit it to one side. His face was lined and tanned a deep brown.

"Thanks kid," Jonah said, taking the reins. "Mitchell, ain't it?"

"Yes," said Mitchell. "How'd you know?"

"Don," he grunted. "Welcome aboard. Hope you make it past the first week. Most don't. Keep yer shooter handy. Haw!"

With this last word, Jonah shook the reins and used his heels to spur the horse forward. In an instant, he was racing out of the station, dust rising behind him. Mitchell just heard him call back "Close the gate", as he spotted five of the ponies heading eagerly forward. Mitchell ran at them, waving his hands to shoo them back. A rangy pony with a blond mane and the look of a mustang evaded him and bolted out of the corral. Mitchell closed the gate and watched helplessly as it cantered around the yard.

"Catch that hoss!" yelled Don, emerging from the office. A few of the men ran out and spread themselves around, trying to corner the runaway. Mitchell made to help them.

"You! Stand by the entrance," said Don. "Don't let him get any further."

Mitchell obeyed, watching in annoyance as the others eventually coaxed the errant pony back into the enclosure.

"Awful sorry, Don." Mitchell said, walking up to his boss.

"What happened?" asked Don.

Mitchell noticed everyone was looking at him. He debated implicating Jonah.

"It was my fault. I forgot to close the gate."

Don tipped his head at Mitchell.

"Good," he said. "I told Jonah to pull that stunt. Wanted to see if you'd rat out one of your fellas. Mind you, he was s'posed to hang back and not let the ponies out. I'll give that Jonah hell when I see him. Can't be too careful around horses. See you don't let it happen again. Alright, you men! You've all got yer dispatches. Time to hit the trail. Mitchell, you watch the gate this time."

Without another word, the remaining men hurried about readying horses and checking their cargo. One by one, they urged their mounts forward, the ponies as eager to get on the trail as the riders. Each gave Mitchell a sympathetic nod or salute as they passed him.

"All right," Don said. "No more pranks today, I promise. Let's put you up on Hellfire. See how you do."

"Which one's Hellfire?" Mitchell asked. There were only a few horses left.

"Why, the escapee we just cornered. Like his name, he's fiery. One of the fastest horses we have, though."

Mitchell eyed the half-mustang. It was standing nearby.

"I'll try. I guess."

"You better. Go on, get yer saddle. You saw how the others did it."

Mitchell grabbed his saddle along with a harness and approached the horse. The animal was lathered from its previous run. Its eyes were wild, and it stamped and flared its nostrils as Mitchell came near. Don watched from the closed gate, not saying a word.

Mitchell took a deep breath and lifted his saddle, aiming for Hellfire's back. The pony ducked its head and butted, sending the saddle flying. Mitchell swore under his breath. Frustration welled in him. He remembered a feisty bull back on his father's farm. His father used to whip it until it got into such a fury nobody could go near it.

"There now," Mitchell said, keeping his voice calm. "No need for that."

He tried to pat the animal's flank. It lowered its head to butt again. Mitchell backed off, hands raised.

"You mind if I get something, Don?"

Don shrugged.

Mitchell ran to the fence, clearing it with a bound. He hurried into the office, down the hall and into the kitchen. Watkins was clearing up. Mitchell grabbed a fistful of sugar from the little bowl he had spotted that morning. Watkins gave him a look but didn't say anything. Mitchell smiled in return and raced back into the corral. On his way back in, he found a saddle brush in the livery rack. He approached Hellfire with the sugar held out. The horse stamped and shook its head, blonde mane flying.

"Come on, now. You be gentle some an' you can have this sweet stuff."

The animal shook its head vigorously. Mitchell felt sure it would bolt again. He squeezed his eyes shut, expecting the worst. After a second, he felt a cold wetness on his palm. He opened his eyes to see Hellfire lapping up the sugar. Mitchell used his other hand to brush down the animal's coat. The horse whinnied with delight.

"Looks like you ain't had a proper rub-down in a while."

After a few minutes of rubbing Hellfire's flank, Mitchell retrieved his saddle. With a lot of coaxing words, he got it up on the pony's back. The harness took longer. Mitchell thought he might have to get more sugar. Finally, he was up on the horse's back, feet in the stirrups.

"Well done, son," Don called. "Hellfire ain't the easiest. Let's see you take a circuit of the corral."

Mitchell urged the horse forward as gently as possible. Hellfire didn't budge. Mitchell tried again. No reaction.

"He don't want to move, Don."

Don chuckled as he walked around to the side of the fence nearest the horse and rider.

"You ain't gonna change this tiger so easily. He's only used to goin' fast. Heyah!"

Don whacked Hellfire's rump as he made the last sound. Hellfire lunged forwards. For an awful few seconds, Mitchell was sure he was going to fall. One hand on the saddle horn, he dug his thighs into the animal's sides, leaning forward to catch the reins tight. Hellfire only slowed marginally. They rode around the corral, tearing up the soft ground.

"You hold on," Don shouted. "It'll get easier."

Mitchell had never ridden like this, galloping at the edge of safety. He thought he might spill off at any moment. The pony was insatiable, galloping at breakneck speed around the corral.

"I reckon you've done enough," Don yelled, after what felt to Mitchell like an eternity.

Mitchell hauled on the reins. Hellfire neighed loudly and came to a sudden stop. He bucked his hind quarters, sending Mitchell flying. Mitchell's last view was of the fastly approaching ground. Then all he saw was blackness with yellow concentric spiked circles.

When Mitchell came to, Don was standing over him. Don's hand rubbed his grizzled chin as he looked down at Mitchell.

"How're you doin?"

Mitchell groaned.

"That was quite a spill. I reckon Hellfire don't like being cooped up. He likes you well enough otherwise."

Mitchell, vision blurred, made out the horse's rump at the water trough.

"We was goin' some fast, weren't we?" Mitchell rasped.

Don barked a quick laugh, bending forward to help Mitchell up. Mitchell shook his head to clear it while Don dusted him off.

"Anythin' hurt bad?" asked Don. "If'n it does, there's a doctor next door at the garrison. I've heard he only knows how to amputate, though."

"I... I'm fine," said Mitchell.

"That's good. Whad'ya say we take a break. Grab your gear and stow it in your locker. That's the chest at the foot of yer bunk. Mebbe you take it easy for a while. I got some papers to see to. Got to get you some bullets too. Doesn't look like you're in much shape for shootin' practice."

"I can... I can practice the bugle."

"Well, that sounds fine. Off you go an' do that. Watkins generally puts out beans aroun' noon."

Don fumbled about, producing a tarnished silver pocket watch.

"Let's see. Less than an hour 'til noon. That'll do. Off you go and tootle on that horn."

Mitchell limped towards the gate. He paused, turning back.

"One thing I gotta ask."

"Go ahead."

"Jonah said most don't make it past the first week. Why's that? Is it they can't ride proper or forgot the oath or fail some other way?"

"Oh no," said Don. "They die on the trail. Either shot or fall off'n break their neck."

Chapter Three
On Probation

The next few days were a blur of activity. Mitchell collapsed in his bunk, exhausted each night. He figured out the bugle after much puffing and spitting, although his jaw ached afterwards. He did fine at shooting practice, firing off rounds at a few cans behind the station. One rider, he suspected Jonah, had put grease on his pistol grip when he had been setting the cans back up. The gun slipped out of his hand and went off, causing Mitchell to hop about terrified as if they had shot him. After the initial shock wore off, he took the ribbing from the others in stride. He spent the rest of the time cleaning out the stables and other odd jobs Don found for him. The only thing he shirked was learning the oath. Mitchell hoped they wouldn't notice if he managed all the other work.

This morning, Don called him into the office after breakfast. As before, Frank was stretched out on the bench.

"How you holdin' up, Stone?" Don asked.

Mitchell noted Don called them by their surnames when he was assigning work.

"Fine," he replied. "Reckon I'm picking things up."

"That's good. Yeah, the others were tellin' me the same. Bit of a lull right now. Frank here's at a loose end. Ain't you, Frank?"

"Yep," said Frank, sitting up.

"I thought," continued Don. "Why don't we get you some decent practice. Head south to Traveler's Rest and come back. That's the first swing station just down from here. We'll make a sport of it. Frank here'll show you the way but it'll be a race back."

"The others are wagerin' on us," Frank said. He gave Mitchell a broad grin.

"Like I said, it's a bit of sport. You foller Frank here all the way down. What is it, about 20 miles to Traveler's Rest? Frank'll bugle them and you swap out fresh horses. Let's see who's the first one back. We'll go easy on you, nothin' to carry in the *mochila*. Whad'ya say?"

"When do we leave?" asked Mitchell.

"I like the sound of that," laughed Frank. "C'mon then."

Mitchell followed Frank out towards the corral.

"Which one d'you want, Mitchell?"

"I'll probably regret it, but maybe I'll ride Hellfire."

"You serious? That demon? All right. Reckon I'll take Tiny. She's big but faster than you'd think."

The two men assisted each other, readying their mounts. Don walked over to the gate to let them out.

"Don't go too easy on him, Frank," Don said. "I seen this boy bust up a saloon brawl."

"I'll keep that in mind. Let's go!"

Frank urged his mare forward. With no urging from Mitchell, Hellfire went for the open gate at top speed.

Before Mitchell could settle in his saddle, they were out on the dusty Salt Lake street. It was busy with morning traffic. Hellfire huffed and surged forward, eager to hit the trail.

"Hold him back a bit," called Frank. "We gotta get out-of-town first."

Mitchell looked over his shoulder at Frank. He knew if he pulled too hard on the reins, Hellfire might buck and spill him again. He still had the bruises from before.

"Easy, Hellfire," Mitchell whispered, leaning forward. "Slow down a bit 'till we clear town."

The horse paid no heed to his soothing words. It raced towards an intersection where a laden cart and a brace of draft horses were passing through. Mitchell only had time to pull as hard as he could on the reins. Mitchell watched horrified as the farmer at the head of the cart yelled at his animals, trying to steer them away from the oncoming rider. They were travelling at enough speed for the cart to swerve precariously on two of its four wheels. Some of its load of dung-laden straw spilled over the side. Hellfire turned at the last minute, narrowly avoiding the cart and horses. Mitchell finally stopped a few yards further along the street and dismounted.

"What in the name of blazes are you boys at?" shouted the farmer, hoping down from his seat. "I don't care what mail y'all are deliverin', you nearly killed me."

"Sorry about that, sir." Frank said, pulling alongside. "His horse is half mustang. The Pony Express'll cover any damages."

"What about my damages?"

Mitchell turned in shock at the familiar voice. Standing on the pavement was Winston: cream suit splattered by dung, hand still bandaged. Alongside him stood a large man with thick knitted brows. The man wore a new tweed suit, too tight on his enormous frame. The farmer took a sideways look at Winston and his companion and hurried back onto his cart.

"No harm done," he muttered. "Best be on my way."

"So," said Winston, ignoring the departing farmer. "This isn't the first time you've destroyed one of my suits, Mr. Stone. Making quite the habit of it, aren't you?"

Mitchell took Hellfire's reins and walked the horse next to Frank.

"Mr. Winston," Mitchell said. "I'm with the Pony Express now."

"I can see that. Joe, this here's the hero in the bar I was telling you about. Stopped me teaching that rat Pierce a lesson."

"That so," the big man said, sticking out his large lower lip. "Good thing I could help ya sort that out later."

"Joe here," Winston said, voice dangerously bright, "had no issue graciously accepting my offer of employment."

"Listen Mister," Frank said. "We're sorry about your suit, but the Pony Express can't wait. My boss will be askin' after us if we're not out and back in good time."

"An' who might that be?"

"Don Russell," Mitchell growled, climbing back on Hellfire. "You can take it up with him."

"Oh, don't worry. I will."

The threatening edge to Winston's words made Mitchell pause. Safe on Hellfire's back, he was about to say more. Before he could, Frank reached over and patted Mitchell's horse.

"C'mon. Let's get outta town before this demon causes any more trouble. You talk to Don, Mister. He'll straighten things out."

Winston said no more, only stared at Mitchell. The riders turned their mounts, pointing them on the main road out of town. Hellfire stomped and shook his head, but Mitchell pulled on the reins hard, letting the fractious horse know who was in charge. They trotted down the street, the buildings thinning out to be replaced by open prairie stretching out to the distant Rockies.

"What'd you do to him?" asked Frank.

"Stopped him killin' somebody," Mitchell replied. "Although I'm not sure it made much difference. He shot at me too."

"Best keep your pistol nearby for a while," Frank said. "I didn't like the look of the big monkey stuffed into that suit beside him."

"Joe, wasn't it? Yeah, I ain't sure exactly all the things Winston is stuck in, but I don't want any part in it."

Frank stared for a while at the wide trail through the dry brush ahead of them.

"I wouldn't worry too much," he finally said. "Pony Express moves us riders around a lot. You might even get a commission to manage a station. They're always lookin' for people."

Mitchell said nothing as they passed a cluster of buildings marking the edge of town.

"Enough talkin'," Frank announced, breaking the silence. "Better make some headway. We want to make Traveler's Rest before sundown. Let's go, Tiny!"

With that, Frank urged his horse forward, making her gallop at a decent clip. Mitchell let Hellfire follow. He sensed the animal's joy at being given free rein again. The day was clear, and they made good time. Mitchell thought the landscape monotonous at first, scarcely noticing it as they galloped along. After a couple of hours he grew accustomed to the pace, observing little details of variation. Sometimes grouse flew out of the brush, disturbed by their pounding hooves. Once, he spotted a group of kangaroo rats leaping away at their approach.

On the back of the horse, it felt as if he were riding a raft down a fast-flowing river. Sometimes, the trail was broken, or they came upon a creek and they had to get the horses to jump. Mitchell thrilled at the brief sensation of weightlessness as the enormous animal beneath him tensed and cleared the obstacle. He laughed aloud each time, and Frank responded with his own excited laughter.

They galloped through a herd of mule deer; they were lithe creatures, twitching their large ears and bolting at the sight of the men on horses. Watching them scamper away to the left, Mitchell was briefly dazzled by the sun nestling into the mountains. He wondered at a rumbling sound he could hear above the clatter of Hellfire's hooves. It took him several moments to realize it was his empty belly.

"Say, Frank," he called. "Ain't we gonna stop an' eat?"

"Eat?" Frank called back. "Pony Express don't stop for picnics. Only a few more miles to the station. We'll grab a quick bite while they get us new mounts."

Mitchell swallowed a few times in quick succession. It was a trick he learned when he was hungry and playing hooky as a kid. He would be absorbed in tracking or fishing, out in the woods, and trick his hunger away. Mitchell could tell Hellfire was tiring; there wasn't the same eagerness for the trail now that the sun was setting. The long shadow of dusk stretched down from the mountains toward them. A worry overtook him. How would he know the way back in the dark? He figured the best thing was to let Frank lead most of the way, to hell with the race.

The sky was a splash of glittering stars by the time they reached their destination. Mitchell had been watching what he thought was perhaps a farmhouse in the gloom ahead when Frank startled him by blowing three times on the bugle. A lantern appeared ahead of them, illuminating a squat stone building with a flat roof. The horses picked up their pace in anticipation of rest ahead. As they approached, Mitchell saw the lantern had been hooked to a pole and a fresh horse with a harness was being led out towards them.

"Looks like we'll have to ride tandem," Frank called back from his lead position. That didn't sound too bad to Mitchell, still daunted at the thought of heading all the way back in the dark.

"Whoa there, Tiny."

Frank brought his horse to a halt under the light. A thin man holding the reins of the replacement horse came forward.

"Howdy Frank," he said. "Nice night. Who's this?"

"This here's Mitchell Stone," Frank said, as Mitchell pulled up alongside them. "Newest member of the Pony Express. Likes ridin' Hellfire, if you can believe that."

"Well ain't that somethin'. Nice to meet you, Mitchell. I'm Harold. Go on in and take a load off while I get you boys a second horse. There's food on the table."

"Thanks Harold. We'll see to Tiny and Hellfire first. We rode them pretty hard down here."

They led their horses over to a long water trough. The animals dipped in their noses, lapping ferociously at the water. Even Hellfire was too tired to make any fuss as Mitchell removed the saddle and bridle. He patted the beast's back.

"That was a good run," he murmured. "Hope we do it again soon."

"Sure you will," Frank said, putting down Tiny's gear. "Tiny'n me have travelled the trail many times, ain't we?"

He fondly stroked the mare's mane.

"No need to tie 'em up," Frank said. He yawned loudly, stretching himself. "They're too tired to go anywhere. Even Hellfire's beat. Harold'll look after them. Let's get some food."

It suddenly struck Mitchell how tired and stiff he was. He longed to eat and sleep as soon as possible.

"They got bunks here for us for the night?"

"Bunks!" exclaimed Frank. "We got about five minutes while Harold gets us a fresh horse. Then we saddle up and head right back up that trail. Those boys back at the station got all kinds of money wagered on us. Be very disappointed if'n we don't come back neck and neck and in good time."

"Agh! I was so glad to make it here, I plain forgot about the race. I'll level with you, Frank. I ain't that sure of the road back. What if I get too far ahead?"

Frank laughed, clapping Mitchell on the back.

"You sure are certain of yerself, ain't you? I'll stop and wait for you if you fall behind."

Mitchell joined in the laughter, secretly relieved.

Within ten minutes they had devoured Harold's food, relieved themselves, and were saddling two fresh mounts. Mitchell had crammed as much of the tepid beans, hard bread, and bitter coffee into his mouth as time allowed. The food and drink settled uneasily in his gut.

"I reckon I'll have an advantage," said Mitchell. "I'm goin' to be expellin' wind hard after them beans..."

"Hah," laughed Frank. "There's another reason for me to stay ahead a' you!"

With that, he shook his horse's reins and galloped north. Mitchell rubbed his new mount's dark mane for good luck, then did the same. He had never ridden in the dark before, especially not at any speed. There was no moon, but the broad canopy of stars provided some illumination for his eyes to grow accustomed to. He focused on the trail ahead and followed as close to Frank as he could. When they came to any obstacle, they stopped and dismounted, leading the animals across.

"Don don't want us to ride so hard as to kill ourselves," Frank said, as they picked their way across one creek. "Or at least not kill one of the horses. Cost him more that way."

As the night wore on, Mitchell started to doze off. Each time, he startled awake, realizing the danger succumbing to dreams would be. At one long, even stretch of the trail, he thought he heard Isabelle's voice. For a moment, he thought she was on the horse with him, hugging his back. He thought he felt her auburn curls against his neck. What was she whispering?

"Careful, Mitch..."

Mitchell, slumped forward on his horse's neck, jerked awake. The horse had slowed to a trot. He looked about in the dark, terrified. Mitchell sat up and hauled on the reins, realizing he didn't even know whether he was heading in the right direction. He halted, listening to the open prairie. He heard faint bird cries and the faint hush of the wind. No sign of Frank. For a long minute, he felt completely abandoned, unsure even where north was. Then he heard the distant clop of horses' hooves.

"Mitchell!" called Frank, his voice carrying in the stillness. "You all right?"

"Frank! I'm over here."

It took a few minutes of shouting in the dark for the men to find each other.

"I'm sorry Frank," Mitchell said when they were back riding together. "I kind of dozed off back there."

"You gotta watch that. Night shift's the worst. Watch the trail even more in the dark."

"You're right. I'll be more careful. I reckon you won the race."

"Never mind about that. Let's get back to the station in one piece first."

The sky had turned a deep azure when they arrived back at Salt Lake. There were few people about as Frank and Mitchell thundered up towards the Pony Express station. At the last hundred yards, Frank pulled up. He waited for Mitchell to draw abreast to his own mount.

"Now we can race."

With a shout, he dug his heels into the horse's flanks and the animal jumped forward. Mitchell did the same. Although Frank had the lead, they were neck and neck pulling into the station. It surprised Mitchell to see Don and a couple of other riders outside waiting for them.

"It was Frank!" one called.

"Naw, it was Mitchell," another replied.

They halted the horses in the front of the men. Both animals were panting heavily from the exertion of the race.

"Whad'ya say, boys?" said Don. "Which one of you won?"

"Frank!" declared Mitchell. "If it weren't for him, I'd still be out there fartin' in the dark."

***

Mitchell was lying in his bunk, trying to force himself to memorize the oath, when Don appeared at the door.

"Got a special delivery job for you," Don said. "After you showed you could handle the trail yesterday. Patron wants us to deliver an urgent parcel only as far as Mountain Dell. First station east of here. Sounds military. Usually they dispatch their own riders, but I guess they're busy. They asked after I'd already sent all the regular riders out. You up for it?"

Anything rather than try to learn this oath, thought Mitchell.

"You bet I am!" he said.

Don handed him a heavy envelope.

"Put that in your *mochila*. They paid double to make sure it gets there before sundown."

Within minutes Mitchell had his gear ready. He debated whether he should take his gun and the bible, but relented and packed them both. Out in the yard, Don had a horse ready for him.

"This colt will do you fine. Be careful now. This is your first time on your own."

Mitchell said nothing, merely giving Don a brisk nod as he busied with saddling his mount. The horse was black with a white diamond on its forehead.

"See you tomorrow then," Don said, turning back to his office.

Mitchell got up on the horse and shook the reins. The black colt trotted towards the gates. This time, Mitchell ensured the animal wasn't going too fast. He wondered how Hellfire was doing and how long before the fiery steed would find its way back to their station. The day was clear, not a cloud in the deep blue sky. Mitchell figured this might make for harder riding, having to squint into the sun as he headed west. He sighed. Don had given him directions on how to get to Mountain Dell. All the same, he was apprehensive of losing his way. His mind focused on his task, he paid little attention to the people passing him. Before he knew it, he was facing the mountains with Salt Lake City to his back. He paused the horse, contemplating the open road ahead.

"Well," he said to his mount. "Guess we better get goin'."

The horse huffed and shook its head a little.

"Tarnation! Sorry horse, I didn't find out your name. I was in such a hurry to hit the road."

The black colt made no reply.

"'Horse' it will have to be. Let's go!"

With that, Mitchell tapped his heels into the animal's side. It was all the signal needed. The black horse jumped forward, eager for the open road. They galloped for about an hour, Mitchell watching the plain slowly break up into foothills. Don had advised him of his first landmark, a low canyon with a thin stream running through it. Mitchell cleared a rise, spotting a gully between two hills. A thin river meandered out of the entrance, bending away to the south.

"Looks like our first signpost, Horse."

Mitchell slowed the animal somewhat when they reached the mouth of the gulch. The trail was strewn with rocks and they had to pick their way. A flash of light caught Mitchell's eye from the northern side of the canyon. He turned. He saw the puff of gun smoke before he heard the crack of the weapon being fired. The boom reverberated around the narrow canyon. Mitchell's chest felt as if someone had hit it with a sledgehammer and he fell to the ground. His horse rose its forelegs, screaming in fright. Spooked, the animal ran back the way they came. Mitchell lay in the dirt. For a moment, he wondered if he was dead. He felt his sore breastbone. *Why was there no blood?* Then he felt the Pony Express bible in his jacket pocket, the leather cover punctured by the bullet.

Mitchell thought fast. Whoever was up there would be down in a few minutes to check on his prey. It took all Mitchell's willpower not to bolt for cover. Instead, he slowly moved his hand down to his holster, finding the pistol's grip. He listened. He could hear loose stone tumbling and cursing as the man stumbled down the gully. Face down in the dirt, Mitchell kept still.

"Hey!" called the man. "You dead?"

Mitchell said nothing. The voice sounded about ten yards away.

"Guess I should have shot yer horse and then you. Now I gotta hunt it down–"

Mitchell spun, turning his gun toward the voice. The man had a rifle in his right hand, down by his side. He was big and burly and wearing a black suit too small for him. In the second it took Mitchell to fire, he realized it was Joe. The big man dropped his rifle, clutching his side. Mitchell grunted, chest still hurting, as he rose and ran over to him. He trained his pistol on the wounded man.

"Did Winston send you?"

"What'ya think? He said to bring back the letters so there'd be no proof."

"You mean you ordered the delivery? So you could get me?"

Joe made no reply. He doubled over, blood pooling around him. Mitchell looked about the narrow canyon.

"You got anyone else here to ambush me?"

Joe shook his head, teeth gritted. His face was pale.

"Jus' me," he grunted. He collapsed onto the rocky ground.

Mitchell shook his head, holstering his gun. He rushed to the fallen Joe, turning him onto his back.

"Here. Get that jacket off."

The suit jacket was tightly buttoned and slick with the man's blood. It took a lot of fumbling to bare Joe's gut. A blackened wound oozed from his pale belly. Joe groaned with pain.

"Quit hollerin!" Mitchell yelled. "I'm tryin' to figure out what to do. Here! Hold that against the... the wound."

He tried to get Joe to press the stained jacket against the bullet hole. Joe screamed at the pain. His words came in between jagged breaths.

"Listen..." he said. "I'm sorry I tried to plug... you. Jus' doin'... my job... for Winston. My ma's name's... Ethel. Can you..."

He never got to finish. Mitchell watched in horror as Joe's face slackened. A rattling sound gurgled out of his mouth and his eyes fixed on a point beyond Mitchell's shoulder. The big man's body lay still. Mitchell stood up, only now noticing his hands were covered in blood. He ran to the creek in a panic, frantically washing the blood off. He stopped and snuck a glance back at the corpse. The big man's wound was still seeping a trickle of black ichor onto the ground. Mitchell retched at the sight, vomiting into the small river.

His first thought was to run. Leave Salt Lake City and the Pony Express. Now that he was... What? A *killer*? He took a series of deep breaths. As he calmed, he reflected it might just as easily have been him dead in the dirt. Horrible as it was, Mitchell had only defended himself. A cold resolve came over him. It wasn't this big lug Joe that had tried to kill him, but that snake, Winston.

Mitchell cupped some fast-flowing water in his hands, splashing his face. The shock of its chill helped him focus on his current situation: he was stuck in the wilderness with no horse and a dead body cooling beside him. He walked over to the body. Joe's heavy face looked calmer now, released from the angry knot he always kept it in. It took Mitchell a few minutes to make himself search the man's pockets. There was a wallet with about twenty dollars and a few cigarette cards. Mitchell frowned as he pocketed the wallet. Was that all it cost to kill a man in Salt Lake? He dragged the body behind a few rocks, sweating with the exertion. He considered covering it up, but thought better of it. Flies were already swarming around. Mitchell walked back towards the lake and picked up the rifle. With one last look around, he headed back along the creek.

It didn't take long to return to the open prairie. His heart sank as he scanned the horizon to the east. There was no sign of his horse. Where would a spooked horse go? Would its instincts tell it to return home? Then he remembered these horses were always moving around and had no fixed home. He looked south along the river and spotted tracks in the soft mud. After an hour of walking, he found the horse amongst a small stand of trees, drinking from the water's edge. The animal was still saddled but its harness was only half on.

"There you are," Mitchell said, putting down Joe's rifle. "All right now. You gotta come on home now."

The black horse raised its head and eyed him with mistrust.

"I know we got shot at. It wasn't nice. You let me catch you an' we can head back to the station. Get proper feed."

Mitchell often found that talking to animals helped calm them, especially fractious ones. He ambled up to the skittish beast. The horse whinnied and made to bolt. Mitchell caught a piece of the right stirrup and hung on. The horse tried to shake him, but he could leverage himself back up on the saddle. The black colt bucked a little, but Mitchell reached forward and patted its neck.

"Shush now. It's all right. You be gentle an' we can get back home. Like I said."

The horse shivered ferociously in acceptance of Mitchell on its back. Quick as he could, Mitchell reattached the harness from the saddle. It was tricky, but he was afraid to dismount, lest he lose the animal again. Eventually, he had him secure enough to ride out of the trees. He looked about for Joe's rifle but couldn't spot it. At least he still had the horse. With a twitch of the reins, he pointed the animal toward town.

***

Mitchell's chest was throbbing by the time he reached the Pony Express station. He had opened his shirt as they rode back and all he could see was a spreading bruise. He wondered if he had broken a bone. Mitchell grunted in pain as he dismounted, taking a moment to steady himself.

"No way a rookie like you could have made it in that time," said Don, stepping out of the office.

"I nearly didn't make it at all," Mitchell said.

"What happened to you?"

"Winston. He got his man to shoot me at that gulch you said to take once I got out by the creek."

"What!"

"Yep. If it wasn't for the good book, I'd be gone."

Mitchell produced the destroyed bible. Don regarded it with a low whistle.

"You lucky so-and-so! I guess there's wisdom in carryin' that around. Why didn't you keep goin'?"

"Keep going! He knocked me off this horse. I had to lay dead in the dirt while he stumbled down and then..."

Mitchell hung his head, at a loss for words.

"What was it, Stone? What happened?"

"I shot him. I had to, Don."

"I understand. That's why we give you men pistols. What'd you do with the body?"

"It's still back there. In the gulch. I reckon I could find it tomorrow. We should get the sheriff..."

Don sucked on his upper lip, considering.

"Hold on. Did you keep anything? The man's gun or anything like that?"

"It was a rifle. My horse ran off and I had the devil's time gettin' him back. Oh. I got this."

He produced the assassin's wallet. Don removed the money, searching it thoroughly.

"Hmm. Can't find anything identifyin'..."

"What about the special delivery?" Mitchell asked. He pulled the single parcel out of the pouch on his *mochila*. He opened the brown paper wrapping it. Inside was a folded copy of yesterday's newspaper.

"Drat!" said Don. "Can you describe the fella who shot you?"

"Big galoot. Thick eyebrows that met. Wore a black suit a couple of sizes too small."

"It wasn't him as ordered the special dispatch. That was a small twitchy runt in a uniform. Could be Winston bribed someone out of the garrison. Point is, we got nothin' to prove Winston had it in for you. I'll bet you anythin' coyotes 'll maul that body beyond recognition by tomorrow morning. All we got is this."

Don handed Mitchell the twenty dollars.

"You keep that. I know it's hard, Mitchell. But 'less you got something concrete to prove Winston wanted you shot, there ain't a lot of use goin' to the law. I wish you hadn't crossed swords with that Winston but he's sure out to get you. An' I certainly don't like the idea of him thinkin' he can take out my riders as he pleases. I got an idea. Get yerself fed and cleaned up. Reckon we'll pay *The Golden Lily* a brief call this evenin'. I know what kind of customer he is and if you don't face them, they'll keep comin' after you."

A couple of hours later, Don and Mitchell strolled down to Winston's establishment. They were both armed. Mitchell's chest still stung, but it wasn't as bad as before. They draped the windows of The Golden Lily in dark curtains. A sign beside the porch read 'Rooms available by the hour'.

"Now, you don't say nothin'," Don said as they approached the door. "The sight of you'll be enough."

Inside, raucous women in white dresses sat at tables with men in various stages of drunkenness. A man in the corner sawed away on a fiddle. It was hard to tell, but it sounded like 'Turkey in the Straw'. The fiddler was sitting beside a little bar where Winston stood. He blanched at the sight of Mitchell at the door.

Don strode into the middle of the room, his hand on his pistol. Mitchell noticed his fellow rider Jonah sitting at a side table with a skinny girl on his lap. Jonah stood up, giving his boss an apprehensive look. The rest of the crowd continued cavorting. Don's lips were pursed in a thin line.

He pulled out his gun and shot one lantern in the corner.

It surprised Mitchell how deadened the sound of a gun was when fired indoors. It was certainly quieter than the sound of the women screaming and the patrons yelling. Mitchell drew his own gun. Jonah pulled his own weapon and took a couple of steps towards them. Don gave Jonah a quick nod, before pointing his gun at Winston.

"Tobias Winston," Don growled, once the noise had settled. "You try to take out a Pony Express rider again and I'll come back here and sort you out proper."

"I don't know what you're talking about," Winston said, eyes narrowed.

"I wouldn't," said Jonah, his gun trained on the deputy.

The deputy raised his hands.

"Now Don," he said. "You know this ain't legal. Mr. Winston runs a reputable business in this town—"

"Shut up," barked Don, not even looking at him. "This is a warning, Winston. You leave my riders alone. I know they bring you a nice bit of business. Everyone knows the Pony Express riders have way more money to spend than any soldier or cowpoke you get. I'll be telling my boys not to come in here for a month. I'll stop them altogether if you don't behave. You hear me?"

"You don't dare—" started Winston, color rising in his cheeks.

Esmeralda stood, shooting Winston an angry look.

"Why, Mr. Russell!" she said, voice reasonable. "I'm sure this is all a terrible misunderstanding. Of course, we value your men the highest of all our customers. In fact, you can let those boys know they can visit here for free for the next while."

"What!" exclaimed Winston.

"Free," stressed Esmeralda, ignoring him. She gave Don a direct look, her green eyes flashing.

"Huh," grunted Don, lowering his pistol. "I'll consider it. If'n you keep *him* in line." He nodded towards Winston. "For now, this place is off limits to the Pony Express. C'mon boys."

Don holstered his gun and turned for the door. Mitchell and Jonah kept their pistols ready as they followed him out, not daring to turn their backs on the room. Esmeralda made a disgusted noise and stormed upstairs, followed closely by a furious Winston. Many of the men sitting at the tables relaxed their hold on their guns. The women beside them relaxed their hold on the men. The fiddler, a knowing grin on his face, started into playing 'Bonaparte's Retreat'.

Chapter Four
Confronting
Standing Bear

"It just seems wrong to me, that's all."

Mitchell stood beside Don at the corral fence. It had been a few days since the incident at *The Golden Lily*. Don didn't reply, he was leaning against the fence staring at the horses.

"That Winston hired someone to kill one of your men. To kill *me*. An' he's getting away with it. You're not even getting the law on him."

"Law?" Don said, raising an eyebrow. "The deputy's his biggest customer. Besides, we saw how to keep Tobias Winston in his place."

"We did?"

Don chuckled.

"Esmeralda. She's somethin', ain't she? Plus, the fellas are all excited at the discount they're gettin' 'cause of you."

"Me? I thought you was keepin' them away from there?"

"Officially. I can't pay these boys as much as I do and expect them to go buildin' churches with it. We got enough churches already in Salt Lake."

Don lifted his hands from the fence and stretched. He grinned at Mitchell.

"What about you? After all you been through, I reckon I can put you on full pay now. Plus, what you got out there in the gulch. What you want to spend your money on?"

"Really, Don? I'm much obliged to you for that."

"Well, that's good," Don said, clapping him on the shoulder. "You forget about Winston an' what happened. I'd stay outta his bookshop though. Or McParland's dive next door where he drinks…"

"I will, Don. I'm none too interested in those places, anyway."

"That so? Fair enough. You still hankerin' after that sweetheart you mentioned before?"

Mitchell looked away, too bashful to say anything.

"All right. Just remember, Pony Express rules say you got to stay a bachelor. While yer in the service, anyway. Speakin' of the rules, why don't we mosey over to the office and get that oath outta the way. Get you on the books proper."

"The oath! I plum forgot about it. Thought I still had time. To… to practice."

"Huh," said Don. "Really not your thing, ain't it. All right. Come on into my office and we'll play dickey bird. We'll go over each line until you have some kind of handle on it."

"Thank you, Don. That'll really help me out."

They retired to the office for a frustrating hour of back and forth.

"Dang!" exclaimed Don. "You surely struggle with this, don't you? It's like tryin' to milk a mustang!"

"I'm real sorry," Mitchell said. "Lemme try once more."

Mitchell stumbled over the words, faltering at the end.

"That'll do!" said Don. "I'm gettin' a headache listenin' to you. Hold on."

He searched about the desk for Mitchell's contract, reading out the words as he signed his name.

"I,... Donald Russell..., manager of... Salt Lake City Pony Express station... do solemnly declare... Mitchell Stone... to have passed his probation period and be a fitting representative of the ideals and morals of the company in... and so on and so forth..."

His voice trailed off, and he stood up straight.

"Phew! I guess you're a full Express rider now. Well done, Mitchell."

"Thank you, Don. 'Specially for the help... with learnin' that off. I've always had difficulty with that kind of thing."

"Don't mention it, son. Main thing's you got there."

"Seein' as how you're so good at paperwork and such. Could I ask you a favor?"

"What's that?"

"Isabelle. The girl back home I told you about. I've been meaning to... write to her. Let her know how I'm doin'. Now that I'm officially a rider, an' all."

"Well, why don't you do that. You could even send it by Express if it's that important."

Mitchell scratched the back of his head, unable to look Don in the eye.

"Thing is, I always rushed any writin' at school an' I don't want to send her somethin' that would put her off. Maybe you could help me out..."

"You want me to write a letter to your girl."

"No, no, no! Just maybe, go over it with me an' help get it finished. Like we just done with the oath."

Don laughed softly.

"How's about we head back to the mess an' grab some lunch. Let's see what we can put together with pen and paper."

"Ah, I don't want the others to know though. They'll only rib me somethin' fierce. Tell you what, I got all this money now. How about we head down to the Palace Hotel? I'll buy you a proper lunch while we do it."

"Hah! Sounds like a good deal to me!"

***

My dearest Isabelle,

I am writing to you from Salt Lake, Utah. I found myself here several weeks ago after working my way from Denver as a cowboy. The land is very dry in this locale and very different from home. The weather tends to be warm and, I am told, will get even hotter when summer comes. Speaking of home, how are you faring? I hope your Mother and Father are keeping well. You can let them know that I have found my place out here as a rider for the Pony Express. You may have heard of them as they are famous across the country. Why, they can deliver a parcel from Kansas city all the way to San Francisco in ten days!

My manager is a very gracious man and has guaranteed me the princely sum of $125 a month as my part in the enterprise. My position is to race a pony through as many stations as I can to ensure the mail gets delivered in a speedy fashion. Do you recall how we used to gallup about on old Dora? She would not last too long on the Pony Express! They *pay top dollar for the finest horses. I have become quite a hand at racing now and have only had to fire my gun once. Although the trail is sometimes broken and unclear, it is pleasant to race about at top speed.*

I wish you could come out here and visit, Isabelle. I do miss you something awful. I hope you aren't too busy at the store. As I am only new to this job, I don't think I can come visit you anytime soon. I dream of the time we can meet again. I will never forget the promise we made that last night before I left. I know it is hard for you to get away, but promise me you'll think of me.

Yours In Affection,
Mitchell Stone
℅ Pony Express Central Office
Salt Lake,
Utah Territory

***

Mitchell was roused from a deep sleep by Don.

"Get up! I got a delivery goin' all the way to Sacramento. Want you to take it as far as Blackrock station. About 160 miles south. Take you a few days to get down there. Best get fed before you head out."

Mitchell mumbled his assent. He was still half asleep by the time he dressed and stumbled into the mess. Watkins presented him with the usual fare: griddle cakes, sow belly, and bitter coffee. He swallowed half a mug, feeling the sour black liquid course down his gullet. Even with that, it still took a minute or two for full wakefulness to arrive. Mitchell used a tarnished spoon to heap the food in after the coffee. He burped and stood up.

"Have a good mornin', Watkins. Won't see you for a while."

Mitchell was used to the taciturn cook by now, and his only response was to remove the empty cup and greasy plate. Mitchell turned and made his way to Don's office.

"Here's the packages," said Don. "I know you've not been as far as Blackrock before, so here's a map as well. I heard from another of the riders that the Paiute have been active, so keep your eyes peeled."

"Paiute?" Mitchell asked, tucking the papers into his *mochila*.

"Yep. Be careful with them. They're a tough tribe, gettin' riled up with all the new settlements in the territory. There's been some stories about their warriors takin' on ranchers lately. I don't know, though. Hard to tell what's story and what's real."

"I got this," Mitchell said, patting his revolver.

"Well. Hopefully you won't have to use it. I'm still of the opinion that it's better for a rider to race off than stand an' fight."

"I know," said Mitchell. "I don't plan on waitin' around. I've had enough of fightin'."

"Ha hah! That was good fun with Watson, all the same. Latest I heard is he's not stirrin' outside. Nobody wants to bodyguard him after what happened."

"That sounds fine to me."

Don's chair squeaked as he leaned back in it.

"Very good. You best be off then. You can rest up at Blackrock for a day or so until there's mail comin' back here. Take Hellfire if you like. He's in the paddock."

"All right."

Mitchell was at the door when Don cleared his throat. Mitchell turned back.

"You be careful out there," Don said. He gave Mitchell an intense look.

Mitchell nodded once and went to find his horse.

***

The first day was pleasant, a cool breeze coming from the mountains. Mitchell made good time, reaching Traveler's Rest before sundown. Harold welcomed him like an old friend. Mitchell realized it must be a lonely existence at the smaller stations.

"Can't you stay for a few minutes?" Harold asked, as Mitchell ate standing next to his horse.

"Naw," said Mitchell. "I want to make good time. I'll see you in a few days. Mebbe I'll stop for a while, then. You look after Hellfire for me."

"You're the real Pony Express now, ain't you? Rather race about with them horses than talkin' to normal folk."

"Ain't that the truth," Mitchell said, smiling wryly as he patted his new horse's nut-brown neck.

He mounted the fresh pony and headed off into the dusk.

It was an uneventful ride to Rockwell's. He stopped to sleep there for a few hours, as he dozed in the saddle again. It was a bigger station than the previous one, and he was glad of the bunk. He made sure the manager there got him up well before ten.

"You sure you rested up enough?" asked the man, as he led the new pony over.

Mitchell's only answer was to hike his saddle over the pony's back and head off.

The weather had changed overnight, and the day was oppressively hot. By mid-afternoon, they reached a tributary of Lake Utah. Mitchell eased up on the pony as he surveyed the broad ford of the river.

"How's about we stop here for a piece," he said. "You and me are both burnin' up in this sun."

He rubbed his neck and could feel by the stiffness of his skin that it was probably bright red. He dismounted and led the horse to the water. The animal drank deeply, glad of the respite. Mitchell took out a handkerchief and dipped it into the gurgling river. The cold thrill of it eased the sting of his neck. Mitchell sighed.

"I reckon we gotta keep goin'," he said to the horse. "Sun's startin' down now, anyway."

The horse looked up from the river and blew its lips in exasperation.

"It's alright for you," he said with a laugh. "You can rest up at the next station. I gotta keep pounding down this trail."

He kept the cloth on his neck as he withdrew the map Don gave him.

"Looks like about another ten miles from this here ford. All right. Enough relaxin'. Sooner we go, sooner you get to rest."

He folded up the map and mounted the pony. The water was shallow at first, but soon came to the animal's knees.

"I hope I got the right spot for crossin'," Mitchell muttered, urging the horse forward.

The water reached Mitchell's own knees, and he wondered if he should dismount and search for a shallower spot. He pulled on the horse's harness, but the animal didn't respond.

"Hey! You fixin' on taking a swim?"

The animal ploughed on. Mitchell had to lift the leather *mochila* to stop the water reaching the mail. For a hair-raising minute he feared both he and the horse were going to float off in the river. The opposite bank looked very distant. His breeches were soaked. The moment of panic passed, and he noticed the pony rise a little from the water.

"I shoulda known," exclaimed Mitchell. "You know this trail, don't you? I probably don't need that old map at all."

The horse whinnied.

"I'll bet you wanted to cool down is all. Well, next time I'll carry this mail higher over water. Don was very particular about it not getting wet or damaged."

Rider and horse travelled on in the waning heat. Mitchell noticed the humidity rising also as his clothes didn't dry out much. His breeches were still damp that night when they reached the next station. He bid the brown stallion goodbye.

"Weather's changing some," remarked the station manager, a wizened old timer with a crooked back. He led a fresh mount over to Mitchell. "Wouldn't be surprised if we got ourselves a storm brewing."

Mitchell looked about at the brown brush extending for miles around them.

"I'm from back east. I thought you got nothing but sun here all year round," he said as he hiked his saddle on the pony's back. The mare was tan-colored with white 'socks'.

"Mostly," agreed the old-timer, standing back. "When we get a storm, we get 'em bad. You take care of Daisy now."

"Daisy?"

The old man gave no response, only shuffled back to his chair by the door.

Daisy and Mitchell galloped on into the night. The mare was strong and wasn't faltering when dawn broke to Mitchell's right. The entire sky was full of low, dull clouds with the ones a lurid crimson where the sun rose. Mitchell slowed the horse to admire the vista.

"At least my sunburn'll have time to heal," Mitchell remarked.

He pulled some dry biscuit from his saddle bag and munched on it for a minute. The plain was flat all the way to the mountains far to the east. It struck Mitchell that he hadn't heard or seen a bird or any other creature for a long while. The brush all about was still and silent. Mitchell shrugged and shook Daisy's reins.

"C'mon! Let's get on with it. Station must only be a couple of hours away."

After a swig from his canteen, he started the horse on the trail again. They rode on. After an hour, Mitchell noticed the wind picking up. To the north, an angry fist of black cloud had formed. Mitchell sighed.

Then the rain started.

It only took a minute for Mitchell to be fully soaked. He wiped his brow and patted the pouches holding the mail. They felt secure, but he daren't risk checking too much. He tried to scan the trail ahead, but the rain obscured his view.

Great curtains of it were coming down, blown about by the wind.

"Whoa, Daisy! We best figure out what's best to do."

Daisy shook her bedraggled blond mane as they came to a stop. A spray of droplets covered Mitchell.

"Thank you, Daisy. But it ain't my fault. Anyway. Just a drop of rain. It'll probably end as quick as it came. Best we not ride in it, though. Case you slip."

He dismounted, nearly falling as one foot slipped from the stirrup. Daisy stood calmly as he reversed the *mochila*.

"Hopefully that'll keep the rain off," Mitchell said. The horse looked away. "Hmm. I'm gettin' too used to talkin' to horses. Hope it ain't a sign I'm goin' crazy."

They trudged on in the damp gloom. Mitchell pondered his recent adventures. He was glad of the chance to work in the Pony Express. It gave him something proper to work on. Stopped him drifting about. His thoughts turned to Isabelle. If she was so dear to him, why did he light out like he had? Sure, her pa hated him, but they could have figured something out. He cursed his mercurial nature, wondering how long before he left the Pony Express.

A flash lit up the sodden prairie, followed closely by a rolling rumble. Mitchell looked north. The clouds there were a witch's cauldron being stirred viciously.

"I' God!" said Mitchell, unconsciously borrowing Don's expletive.

Another flash and rattle of thunder. This time he saw the lightning fork down from the sky: a sudden river of quicksilver. He shivered. He was cold and overcome by sudden worry. What if one of them were hit by lightning?

Wasn't it dangerous to be the only thing standing for miles around? He looked all around them, spotting a break in the plain to the south. It was only a couple of low hills with a few scraggly trees.

"C'mon Daisy. Change, of course. This storm ain't letting up."

Horse and man slogged through the muck, heads bowed from the rain and wind. The lightning and thunder were both coming at the same time now. The storm clouds above them were murderously dark. At every strike, Mitchell feared they were done for, the promise of shelter so distant. He tried to quicken their pace, but it was heavy going. He would dearly have liked to ride there, but feared the horse might topple on the suddenly uncertain terrain. The wind was picking up too, blowing hard into their faces.

They trudged on for what felt like hours. Mitchell lost all track of time. He was staring at the ground ahead, pulling Daisy forward, when he noticed the rain stop abruptly. He looked up. With relief, he spotted the clouds ahead had lightened. He straightened up and wiped the rain from his brow. They were going to be alright.

Then he heard it — a rumbling like the opening of the gates of hell. Initially, he thought it might be more thunder, but it was too prolonged. He looked behind. About two hundred yards away, the cloud had formed into a low black funnel. It looked like an enormous black rope dropped from the sky.

Tornado.

He had heard of them. They weren't unusual back in Kansas. He watched, mouth agape, as the twister danced closer, brush and debris being sucked heavenward at its base. The wind was so strong, the sound of it hurt his ears. Daisy bucked and stamped, eyes rolling with fear. Mitchell gripped the reins as tight as he could.

"Let's go, Daisy!" he yelled.

There was nothing for it but to run.

At some point, Mitchell and the horse separated. The animal was too terrified and the wind too fierce. Mitchell grabbed the *mochila* as the horse tore away.

"Come back, Daisy! You'll be—"

His futile words were lost to the howling wind. Mitchell ran for his life. At one point, he felt the ground fall away beneath him. He couldn't see the swirling vortex anymore, just clouds of dust. Was he being sucked up to the sky? He could make out the stand of trees a few yards away. He plunged forward, falling on his hands and knees and crawled, the leather *mochila* between his teeth. With a huge effort, he reached a tree and clung to it.

Suddenly, the wind calmed. He looked up. Cloud and brush were whipping all about, but Mitchell could see a circle of blue sky right above, an impassive eye staring down at him. He realized he only had a minute before he was back in the worst of it. He stared about, spotting a few large boulders amongst the trees. It looked like there was a gap between them. He dashed for the crevice, surprised to find a small cave going back several yards. The wind got more violent as he neared the entrance. Exhausted, he jumped forward. A flying branch glanced off the back of his head. Dazed, he squeezed through the cave entrance, collapsing onto the rocky soil. He passed out there in the dark. Outside, the roaring wind called for him, angry it had lost a victim.

***

Mitchell woke to a lance of sunlight breaking into the cave. He sat up with a start, shaking his throbbing head, groaned and collapsed back. He laid there for a long while: vision blurred and head hammering.

Eventually, he recovered enough and sat back up, squinting to take in his surroundings. The light illuminated the rock across from him. It was pale red stone with faint ochre figures. To Mitchell's eye, they could either be freshly painted or carved thousands of years ago. The long, tapered men carried spears or clubs and were clustered about an oversized sun. In Mitchell's confused state, they appeared to be moving. He rubbed his eyes. *What kind of cave is this?*

He stood, noticing a mound of medium-sized stones. Mitchell rubbed the back of his head, feeling the sizable lump there. He walked over to the entrance, amazed to find the *mochila* there, crumpled but still intact and checked the pouches. Incredibly, everything was as before. He crouched and exited the cave mouth, surveying the landscape. The sun was as bright as a few days ago and the air was fresh and pleasant. He could hear a bird twittering nearby. It uprooted several of the trees or had major limbs exposed — the only signs of the previous day's destruction.

Mitchell rubbed his jaw, wondering what to do next. He thought there might be some biscuit left in one pouch and re-entered the cave. The biscuit was soggy and stale, but still edible. He munched on it for a while, his vision steadying. Feeling a little better, he crouched down to better explore the back of the cave. Mitchell noticed the stones were smooth and...he jumped back in shock. The pile was a dusty collection of skulls.

Mitchell grabbed the leather *mochila*, scurrying out as if he had discovered a nest of rattlesnakes. He backed away from the little cave entrance, afraid some malign spirit was going to leap out after him. Staring at it, he felt a tingling sensation on the back of his neck. For a second, he thought it was just his sunburn, sensitive to the mid-day sun. Then he heard a horse snort. Mitchell turned around slowly.

Four men faced him on horseback, one holding Daisy's reins. She looked none the worse for wear, although her saddle was nowhere to be seen. The men had long black hair, which they kept in ponytails. They wore battered hats and other pieces of western clothing, and handwoven scarves and animal skins. Some wore intricate beadwork. Two of them held rifles.

"Ah, hello," Mitchell said. "I think that's my horse."

There was no response.

"Was this?" Mitchell gestured back at the cave. "Was this your graveyard? I needed shelter from that storm. I'm sorry if I shouldn't have..."

Mitchell's voice faltered. One brave had lifted his rifle and pointed it at him.

"Don't! Don't shoot. Look. Here's my gun." He reached for his colt.

The oldest looking man barked something. The brave with the rifle sighted along the barrel at Mitchell.

"No, no! I'm just going to put it down. It's soaked from all the rain, anyway. I'm not even sure it'll fire. See... Puttin' it down now."

With a lot of hand motions, he removed the revolver, holding the hilt with two fingers to place it on the ground. He straightened back up and raised both hands high. The older warrior muttered something, and the others laughed. The youngest came off his mustang, unwinding a rope from his shoulder. He grabbed Mitchell's hand and started tying it. Mitchell considered making a run for it but thought better of it. The other warrior still had a rifle pointed at him. In a minute, they tightly bound his hands. The other end of the rope was around Daisy's neck.

"Not sure how I'm goin' to get on Daisy's back with my hands tied."

Mitchell made to mount his horse. The rifleman yelled something, and he backed off, realizing they meant for him to walk. The oldest chuckled and said a few more words. Then they rode off, leaving Mitchell and the youngest. He had picked up Mitchell's revolver, admiring it.

"You be careful with that," Mitchell said. "Liable to blow your eye out."

The brave paid Mitchell no attention, putting the gun in a saddle bag slung around his horse's neck. He also took the *mochila* and studied it. Shrugging, he draped it over Daisy's back. He mounted his own pony bareback and took both Daisy and his own horse's reins.

"Hee-yah!" said the young man, urging them forward.

The rope jerked taut and it forced Mitchell to jog to keep up. Mitchell noticed the other horse's ribs stuck out from lack of feeding. After a while, the animal slowed the pace, something Mitchell was glad of. The native said little as they plodded along. Every once in a while, Mitchell might stumble and cause Daisy to falter. The young man would fall back and yell something until Mitchell was back on his feet.

"Look, can't we rest," Mitchell asked after an hour. "I can't feel my arms and next time I fall I might break one of 'em."

The brave looked back, a bored look on his face.

"Fall. Break. Arm." Mitchell said. His voice rasped with desperation.

There was no stop, although their pace slackened.

The sun was low in the west when they reached a cluster of hide-covered *tipis* near a river. A few young children stopped scrabbling in the dirt at Mitchell and his captor's approach and stared at them. They didn't run forward or call out. Mitchell, head swimming from his ordeal, still had enough presence of mind to wonder at their hollow-eyed expressions. The young warrior made a show of trotting forward the last twenty yards into the clearing at the center of the village. Mitchell struggled to keep up. He felt sure he would vomit with exhaustion. The brave pulled the horses to a halt and Mitchell collapsed, knees going from under him.

The young warrior untied the rope from Daisy's neck and threw it near Mitchell. Without another word, he gathered the bridles of both horses and led them to a rough enclosure past the dwellings. Mitchell sat up, trying to rub sensation back in his hands. He considered his options; hungry and exhausted, he realized he didn't have too many.

A flap opened in a nearby *tipi*. Mitchell had a brief glimpse of a small cooking fire within. A few men exited. One was the older man that mocked Mitchell earlier. Behind them came a heavy man. He wore no European clothing, only hides ornately decorated with beads. He had large feathers in his hair and his eyes were black with charcoal.

"You!" he said, standing over Mitchell. "What's your name?"

"M... Mitchell. I'm sure glad to hear someone speak English. I'm with the Pony Express—"

"Be quiet! My name is Standing Bear. I am the medicine man for this tribe. I speak your tongue because I learned it from one of your preachers. Mister Smith." Standing Bear spat out the name. "He came to our tribe and tried to teach us. Many got sick from his bad medicine. Many got sick and died."

"I'm sorry to hear that. Look. I don't want to cause any problem for you. Maybe I could talk to someone about helpin' you out. Find you some food or somethin'."

"We are done with your help!"

Standing Bear turned to the other men and spoke to them in Paiute. The older one spoke at length in response. Standing Bear glared at him.

"What is this? You were in our sacred cave?"

"There was a tornado. I had to hide from it. I thought I was done for."

"We believe the land all about us is God. Not the one in heaven Mister Smith wanted us to follow. The spirit of the land wanted you gone."

"I don't know nothin' about that," Mitchell said.

"I must speak with my chief about what to do with you. It is plain the spirits wanted you to join them. He has other plans but..."

The older man interrupted the shaman. Mitchell thought this must be the chief. Voices rose in argument. Mitchell felt weak again, his legs buckled. The Paiute men stopped talking. One called behind him. A middle-aged woman appeared, her black hair streaked with gray. Her cheeks were gaunt. She asked a question of the braves and the chief replied, pointing at another *tipi*.

"Running Deer will take you to the sickness tent and feed you," Standing Bear growled.

"Thank you," Mitchell said. "I'm mighty grateful. I'll just rest up some an' I'll be gone tomorrow."

The woman reached down for his rope and jerked it, indicating a dilapidated *tipi* at the edge of the village.

"Gone?" the shaman said. "Yes. You will be gone."

"That's... mighty kind of you."

Standing Bear grinned at Mitchell, his smile cold. Mitchell noticed the man's face was full and fat, the only one here that wasn't lined with hunger.

"Perhaps you will join Mister Smith in your heaven."

"What do you mean?" Mitchell asked.

"We must have a *pauwau*. To decide the best way to send you to him."

Mitchell gulped as Running Deer led him away.

"Send me?" he asked. "I don't..."

"Kill you!" snapped the shaman. "We must decide the best way to kill you."

Chapter Five
The U.S. Infantry Outpost

The interior of the *tipi* was dark and smelled of sickness to Mitchell. A few bodies lay here and there under hide blankets. The middle of the dim enclosure had a small fire with a cooking pot over it. The fire was a few red embers surrounded by blackened stones. Running Deer motioned for him to sit by the fire.

"Sit?" Mitchell said, looking about. "But there's nowhere…"

She frowned at Mitchell before sitting on one mat, legs crossed underneath her. Mitchell's eyes widened, and he forced himself to copy her. Even if he weren't near exhaustion, he would still have squirmed with the struggle of sitting that way. He gave it up and splayed his legs to one side. Running Deer looked askance at Mitchell. Her lined face cracked a brief smile, and she said something. Nobody else in the room responded. She leaned forward to the rope around Mitchell's wrists. With a few expert twists, she untied him.

"Thank you kindly," Mitchell said, rubbing his rope-burned wrists.

Running Deer took brief notice of his gratitude, reaching instead for the blackened pot perched over the fire and stirring it. Taking a wooden bowl from alongside the little hearth, she ladled out some stew and presented it to Mitchell.

"Oh! That's fine. There's a lot of hungry lookin' people around here. Why don't you give it to them kids outside?"

She narrowed her eyes at his words and pushed the bowl insistently at Mitchell. Mitchell gulped and took it from her. He was famished, but also wondered whether he could make himself eat this strange food. He took the wooden spoon provided and tried a tentative bite of the venison stew. It was delicious, and he devoured it in a few minutes. Running Deer watched him, head cocked to one side. He looked up, scraping the last remnants from the dish.

"That was mighty tasty. Thank you."

Saying nothing, she took the bowl from Mitchell. With a jerk of her head, she showed a vacant spot for him to sleep. Mitchell nodded and lay down on the pile of hides there. An old man slept nearby. His soft rattling snoring sounded unhealthy up close.

"Hope I don't get sick lyin' down here," Mitchell mumbled, tucking himself in.

Exhaustion got the better of him and he fell into a deep oblivion, despite his unusual surroundings.

***

Mitchell was half-awake when the *tipi* flap snapped open, dazzling him as sunshine flooded into the space. Blinded, Mitchell half-rose from his spot.

"Who's there?" he mumbled.

The interior darkened briefly as a burly form blocked the entrance. When Mitchell could see again, he felt his head jerked back roughly as someone tugged on his hair. Fear brought him fully awake, feeling the coldness of a blade against his neck. Standing Bear was inches away from his face.

"I could kill you now," said the shaman. "The spirits would be happy if I did."

"I... I... There must be something we can—"

"Silence!" barked Standing Bear. "No words!"

He stood and dragged Mitchell with him, knife still held near.

"Outside!"

Mitchell complied, stumbling a little as they shoved him towards the entrance. He blinked in the morning sunlight, slowly realizing a larger group of warriors were standing in a semi-circle around him. Several held tomahawks or rifles. Mitchell calculated his chances of survival were he to try to run. He felt sure one of them would dash forward and take him within seconds.

Standing Bear stepped out and said something in Paiute. It didn't take any translation to hear the anger in his words. The chief replied quietly and at length. When he fell silent, Mitchell gave a sideways glance to the furious shaman.

"My chief says you are to be spared. Although I have told them of the wish of the spirits to have you removed from this plain. Our people are starving and sick and the spirits need satisfaction for your crimes. Instead, he wishes to return you in exchange for *supplies*."

Standing Bear spat out the last word with disdain. It took Mitchell a few moments to absorb that he wasn't about to die, so sure was he of his impending demise.

"You... You will not kill me?" he asked.

Standing Bear remained silent, grinding his teeth in anger. The chief spoke some more, directing a pair of warriors towards the horse enclosure.

"Can I... am I getting Daisy back too?"

Standing Bear made a disgusted noise.

"She is too valuable to trade. We will take you away from here and returned to your tribe. If the trade is favorable. If you ever return here again, I *will* see the wishes of the spirits are met."

Standing Bear shoved Mitchell, nearly knocking him to the ground. He spoke to the assembled tribe in a low voice. To Mitchell's ear, it sounded like an incantation, and not a good one. The shaman raised his knife several times, stabbing the air. Abruptly, Standing Bear turned and walked off. Some warriors murmured to each other, their eyes on the departing shaman. The elderly chief ignored the display, gazing all the while over Mitchell's head.

The pair of young braves returned on horseback. One brave took out a rope and threw it onto the ground near Mitchell. He pulled out Mitchell's revolver from a pouch and pointed it at him. It was the young man who had dragged him all the way here.

"Oh, it's you, is it?" Mitchell said. He folded his arms. "Well, Buttercup, if you think you can haul me around the bush again, you can shoot me now. Seein' as I'm so valuable 'n all."

Mitchell wasn't sure why he called the brave Buttercup. Maybe because he was the furthest thing from a pretty little flower that Mitchell could imagine. Buttercup scowled and shook the gun some more, making threatening noises. Mitchell stood his ground. One brave standing beside the chief laughed and suggested something. The chief nodded his assent. Buttercup stuck out his jaw angrily, but bowed quickly before walking off. He returned with a scrawny looking gelding. Like all the horses, there was no saddle on its back. It amazed Mitchell to see his battered *mochila* draped over the animal's back.

"Horse!" insisted Buttercup, waving the pistol again.

"You be careful with that gun," Mitchell warned, approaching the thin pony. "Well. This ain't Daisy, but it'll have to do."

With little preamble, most of the assembled braves mounted their own horses. Soon, there were twenty of them ready to leave. Buttercup quickly fashioned a hackamore from his rope and put it over the muzzle of Mitchell's horse. He mounted himself and tugged on the rope.

"You sure enjoy hauling me around, don't you?" Mitchell said, holding onto the crude bridle to steady himself.

Buttercup gave Mitchell a look and barked something in reply. Although Mitchell couldn't understand, he heard the sneering contempt in his captor's voice. He decided it best for him to remain quiet for the duration of their journey. The warrior who suggested he have a horse raised his rifle and called out to the assembled men. The mounted warriors responded with a fervent cry, an ululating screaming that raised the hackles on Mitchell's neck. The leader spurred his horse forward, and the mounted Paiute warriors followed. Roaring their war cries, they left the chief and near-empty village behind in a cloud of dust.

Mitchell was glad to be on the move again, although bareback riding took a lot of getting used to. Every ten minutes, his weak pony would falter and fell back. Buttercup would respond by angrily hauling on the rope, dragging them forward. Each time Mitchell nearly slipped off, his tight grip on the rough rope the only thing stopping him from being dashed onto the rocky plains.

Several hours of riding this way and Mitchell was fading fast. The gaps of time between his pony falling back came more frequently, and Buttercup's fury kept increasing. Mitchell felt sick to his stomach from the ordeal. His fingers were numb from being clenched for so long. He called out a few times as he nearly fell, but nobody paid him any heed.

"I believe," he muttered to himself. "They won't get much value for whatever's left of me when we get there."

In his delirium, Mitchell kept fixating on his mother's one good rug. He imagined the ruby red carpet just out of arm's reach, beyond the scrub pony's ears. He recalled how his mother would hang it on the line and whack it repeatedly, even when all dust was gone from it. He used to watch her silently, wondering why she kept hitting something she prized so much.

Mitchell looked up from his horse's mangy neck, realizing that they had come to a stop. Ahead of them was a low wooden outpost, surrounded by a palisade of sharpened logs. A single flag wafted in the light breeze. Mitchell was never so delighted to see the 32 stars and 13 stripes. The

Paiute warriors conferred, gesturing across to the outpost. Eventually the leader rode up to Mitchell.

"You come!" he announced, taking the rope from Buttercup.

"Gladly," said Mitchell.

"Trade or kill," said the brave, producing his tomahawk.

"I understand," he said, raising his hands. "I'll behave."

The leader studied Mitchell, his dark aquiline eyes studying him. Finally, he nodded to another brave and the three of them trotted to the entrance to the palisade. As they neared the structure, a shot rang out.

"Who goes there? This is a U.S infantry outpost. We are heavily armed here."

"Hello," Mitchell called back. "My name is Mitchell Stone. I'm a Pony Express rider. These Indians found me after the storm. They want to trade."

"Trade? What do they have?"

"Me. I do believe they'll kill me if you don't bring out some supplies. Their tribe is starving and sick."

A long silence ensued. The braves stared at the wooden enclosure, stony-faced. Mitchell wondered how long he had before their patience wore out.

"All right!" came the voice from behind the enclosure. "We have some supplies we can spare. They've got to let you go first."

Mitchell swallowed. He looked at the leader, pointed at himself, and made a gesture of walking toward the entrance.

"No!"

The Paiute rose his hand and brought it down fast. The remaining braves, holding back out of gunshot, galloped down to their position. The leader gave Mitchell a meaningful look.

"Listen," Mitchell called out. "They've got twenty braves here and they don't mind comin' in and takin' everything. Maybe you could lower down them supplies over the fence an' then they'll let me go."

"What did you say your name was?"

"Stone. Mitchell Stone. With the Pony Express."

"Stone? All right. Any of them understand us?"

"Some. Not much, far as I can tell."

"Fine. But don't trust the buggers. There's only ten of us in here and I reckon they know it. We'll put some stuff down, feed, blankets, even a few old flintlocks. You've got to come get it. They get too close, who knows what'll happen."

Mitchell looked over at the leader who was studying him again.

"Feed. Clothes. Guns," he spoke slowly. "I'll get it."

The leader gave a brief nod, turning away to call a brave over. He spoke low, issuing instructions. The other warrior pointed a rifle at Mitchell, motioning at him to dismount. Mitchell took his time, joints stiff from the long ride. He stood and took a few steps forward.

"Come on!" Mitchell shouted. "I think their patience is wearin' out."

A barrel appeared at the top of the fence. A rope lowered it down. Rifles trained on him, Mitchell walked up to it. Inside were some small sacks of grain, blankets and a few rusty revolutionary era long-guns.

"Is that all you got?" shouted Mitchell.

"What? Are you their dealer now, Stone?" came the reply.

"Just want to get out of here in one piece," muttered Mitchell to himself.

The barrel was too heavy to lift, so he rolled it back to the tribe. The leader looked in, making an unimpressed face. He grabbed Mitchell.

"More!" he said.

"More? Didn't you hear him? That's all they got."

"Fire water," insisted the leader.

"Fire..."

Realization dawned on Mitchell and he called out.

"Whiskey! Do you have any whiskey in there?"

Mitchell could make out faint laughter.

"You drive a hard bargain! Lucky for you, turns out we have a couple of barrels. This time, I'll roll it out the gate and leave it open a crack. You come in and we'll shut it behind you."

Mitchell looked at the leader. He kept his expression calm.

"Fire water. Yes. I'll get."

The leader narrowed his eyes with suspicion but made no move to stop Mitchell. Mitchell walked once more towards the high wooden gate. He was a few paces away when it opened and a whiskey barrel rolled out. Ducking low, Mitchell ran past it and into the enclosure. A yell and a shot followed him. A man in a navy blue Union uniform quickly slammed the bolt behind him. Outside, there was much whooping from the Paiute. Not another shot was fired, though. Mitchell looked up to see another soldier on a platform above them, rifle trained on the braves.

"Lieutenant!" the soldier called down. "They're comin' close. Should I open fire?"

The officer considered. He had a thin moustache to disguise his youthful face. Mitchell thought he couldn't be much older than himself.

"Hold!" called the officer. "We shoot one of them and they'll swarm the place. Stone, do you know how to fire a rifle?"

"Yes, sir!" Mitchell said. "Pony Express taught me to shoot."

"Here." He handed Mitchell a Springfield. "Get up on that platform with private Harley."

Mitchell complied. He did a quick scan of the interior. There was only a single one story wooden building, a few horses and a single small artillery piece perched above two large carriage wheels.

"Lieutenant, I thought you said there were ten of you?"

The lieutenant flashed a smile.

"Don't believe everything you hear, Stone. Besides, I believe they speak English far better than they let on."

Outside, the yelling subsided. Aiming the rifle, Mitchell dared to look out over the fence. The Paiute were sauntering away, their backs to the enclosure. Two braves rolled the barrel of whiskey.

"I reckon the whiskey did the trick," Mitchell said. "I don't know how they'll get it all the way back to their village."

The lieutenant had joined them on the platform and was looking over Mitchell's shoulder at the scene below.

"Oh. I expect that'll be drank up before too long. At ease, Harley."

The soldier grunted and stood up.

"Are you sure it's safe, sir?" Harley said. "You never know with these Paiute."

"I think the whiskey will probably keep them passive for a while. But we will take turns keeping watch until the reinforcements return."

He turned to Mitchell.

"So. Mitchell Stone of the Pony Express. It sounds like you have quite a tale to tell. The name's Weed. Lieutenant Randolph Weed of the Fourth U.S. Artillery. It's a terrible name, I know. My family's from Connecticut. It's common there. Common as a weed, you might say."

Mitchell smiled, shaking the lieutenant's outstretched hand.

"I'm much obliged to you, Lieutenant Weed. My name's common too, I suppose. Common as stone."

"Seems we have a lot in common then. Won't you come down to the bunkhouse and tell me your story? I'll bet you're hungry."

Mitchell looked back over the palisade. Outside, the prairie stretched away quietly, the Paiute dispersed. Mitchell noticed something in the dirt.

"That sounds good. Ah. I just have to do one thing."

Mitchell jumped down the ladder that led up to the platform and unbolted the large gate.

"Hey!" shouted Harley. "Where's he goin'?"

"I don't know," Weed replied, shielding his eyes against the setting sun to watch Mitchell pick up something.

Mitchell reappeared, pulling the gate shut behind him. He had the crumpled *mochila* slung over his shoulder. He patted it, looking up to the soldiers.

"Pony Express always delivers the mail," he said. "I reckon this was a last present from Buttercup. Now then. What was that you were sayin' about food?"

***

Mitchell ended up staying at the army outpost for a few days. Lieutenant Weed was good company and enjoyed Mitchell's stories of his life as a rider with the Pony Express. Mitchell figured the man was starved for company, being the only officer here. Besides, Harley said little. Before his posting in Utah, he had been fighting as part of the war against the South and sometimes stared off into the distance with a haunted look.

"How come there's only two of you out here?" Mitchell asked over supper one night. "Ain't it dangerous?"

"Army's stretched thin," said Weed. "With all the fighting back east. Did you ever think of enlisting yourself? Army could use good men like you. Be less dangerous than racing through Indian territory for fun."

"I don't know," said Mitchell. "I thought about it. But I've never been one to settle on anything for very long. Suits me to be racin' around. Plus the money's better."

Weed chuckled and shook his head.

"Money's no good if you've got an arrow in your back. Anyway, we've got reinforcements coming from Fort Laramie tomorrow. Now that the Paiute have got more militant, attacking settlements all about the territory. We need to show more of a presence."

"Any chance some regiment'll be heading up to Salt Lake?"

"I will! I'll see you returned to your precious Pony Express. Never do to deprive them of their finest rider."

"I don't know about that," said Mitchell. "Thank you, though. I appreciate you comin' back up with me. They must think I'm long dead."

"Oh, don't mention it," Weed made a dismissive gesture. "I need to speak to the General. Besides, the Express is an important part of opening up Utah. God knows we need to keep this country stitched together!"

Mitchell just nodded, preferring to avoid discussion of the civil war.

"Plus," Weed continued, swallowing back his glass. "We're running out of whiskey! Know of any good places in Salt Lake, or is it as dry as its name?"

"I know of a couple of places I have to stay away from."

"That sounds interesting!" Weed said, a twinkle in his eye. "I was hoping you got up to more things than just talking to your horse as you wandered about in the wilderness chased by savages."

Mitchell made a quick smile, sipped from his own glass, then filled Weed in on the tale of his run-in with the owner of *The Golden Lily*.

"Quite a story," Weed said. "I'd say you're not finished with that character yet."

"I know it," Mitchell agreed. "Hard to say who to worry about more, him or Esmeralda."

"Hmm. Maybe I could go in and reconnoiter the situation."

Mitchell laughed.

"That's mighty kind of you to offer."

The next day, a distant bugle call woke them before dawn. Mitchell stumbled out of his bunk and dressed quickly. Outside, he found Harley standing at attention at the gate as fifty troops marched in. Weed was conferring with a portly man. He looked up and motioned for Mitchell to join them.

"...and this is Mitchell Stone. He's had some hair-raising adventures amongst our friends the Paiutes. Stone, this is Sergeant Barnes. Barnes will take over here."

"Pleasure to meet ya'," said Barnes. "How d'you do it? Survive them savages. Is it true they eat their own kind?"

"I didn't see too much of that," Mitchell said with a shrug. "Although I had some of their stew. It was mighty tasty too."

The Lieutenant laughed.

"There you are, Barnes," he said. "You'll be dining with these Paiute in no time. Having them over for supper."

"I doubt that," Barnes said, his expression grim.

"In any case," Weed continued, ignoring the sergeant's tone. "We'll let these men settle in. A small contingent of us will continue north by horse later in the morning."

"Very good, sir."

"Best gather your belongings, Stone," Weed said. "Don't want you to forget your precious mail."

"You still have the mail after being kidnapped?" asked Barnes, eyes bulging with disbelief.

"That's the Pony Express way," Mitchell said with a smile.

***

The journey back took longer than expected. The army horses were slow, as they were more used to hauling artillery pieces. They also had to take a detour to another outpost. By the time Mitchell was riding back into Salt Lake, a whole three weeks had passed. The Pony Express station was a welcome sight. Lieutenant Weed halted outside the gate, the brass of his uniform's buttons glinting in the sunlight. He had spent some time in a local barber's changing into his best uniform and getting his hair and whiskers shaved. Mitchell and the other men had waited outside impatiently.

"Here we are, Mitchell," Weed said. "Sorry it took so long getting you back home."

"Not at all, Lieutenant. I feel like I know the territory much better now. And I owe you my life."

Weed made a dismissive sound.

"Pshaw, that's nothing. Glad to. Who knows? Without your quick thinking, those Paiutes might have figured out how lightly garrisoned we were."

Mitchell dismounted, retrieving his *mochila* from the horse's saddle.

"All the same," Mitchell said. "I'm much obliged. Maybe we can meet up again when you've everything settled in there."

Mitchell motioned his head towards the large garrison across the street.

"That sounds good to me," Weed said. "Although, I think I'll have a fight on my hands to get the troops we need. All going well, I'll probably end up down in Fort Laramie after this. Pony Express comes through there regularly. Why don't you drop by some time you're racing through?"

"Will do. Thank you, Randolph."

"You look after yourself, Mitchell."

Mitchell turned and walked through the gates. Inside, the corral only had a handful of ponies. He walked up to the fence.

"Hellfire! They got you cooped up in there."

He went to the side of the corral where the horse was scratching against the fence. Mitchell rubbed the horse's neck, chuckling when it whinnied with delight.

"I' God! It's the dead come back to life!"

Don stepped out of his office, removing his cap in disbelief.

"Howdy, Don. 'Fraid I didn't deliver this on time."

Mitchell held up the battered mail.

"What the hell happened, son? Never mind that mail or the horse. Come into my office and tell me everything."

Mitchell followed Don back inside. The office was empty apart from the pair of them.

"It's a bit of a story," Mitchell said, sitting down. "I was goin' fine until I got hit by a twister. North of Crittendon, I reckon it must have been."

"We had word over a week ago, sayin' you didn't show up there. A twister? How'd you survive that?"

"I nearly didn't. I got lucky. Found shelter in some Paiute tomb. Full of skulls."

"You did not!"

"Sure did. Crazy drawings on the walls. Felt like it had been there since before the Flood. Anyway, I made it through the night but woke up the next day with a bunch of angry braves on the doorstep."

Don just shook his head. Mitchell continued.

"They hauled me back to their village on the end of a rope. Must have been a day travelin' by foot. When I got there, I was sure they were goin' to finish me off. Their head medicine man sure wanted to. Next day, though, the chief spared me. Said I was better for bargaining with."

"Said? What, you speak Paiute now?"

Mitchell chuckled.

"Mebbe. I reckon you'll learn any language if your life depended on it."

"So what happened then?"

"We rode up to an infantry outpost. I didn't know it, but they only had two men in there. One of them's the Lieutenant. Anyway, had to wrangle some to get them to exchange me for supplies. It was a barrel of whiskey that convinced them in the end. I think if the Lieutenant hadn't thought of that, we were all done for."

Don gave a low whistle.

"That's some story. What's this Lieutenant's name?"

"Randolph Weed. I got to know him well on the way back up here."

"Don't know him. Must be new," Don said, leaning back in his chair. "Quite a story, Mister Stone. You certainly are a lucky one. Let's have a look at that parcel."

Mitchell handed it over. Don inspected it and gave a low whistle.

"Whoever Mr. Ebeneezer Warpole is. He won't have any idea what a story's behind this here clump of documents takin' such a long time makin' its way to him."

"I ain't finished yet. I aim to get back out there an' deliver it. Tonight if'n you'll let me."

Don shook his head.

"You're real Pony Express, ain't you?"

Don put the package down on his desk with a sigh. "Listen, Mitchell. A few things have happened while you were gone. When word got out that you weren't comin' back, Frank, Jonah and a few of the boys thought it might be because Winston wanted to settle that score with you. They cornered him at *The Emerald Isle*. I guess it got a little hot. Shots fired. This time Winston got what was comin' to him. He's laid up with a bullet in his side. Deputy got all worked up about it. Had to send the boys away to other stations. Jonah back east and Frank out west to a new station we're settin' up at Egan Canyon. Frank don't want to manage it for too long, though. Now that you're back, I'm thinkin' I might get you to do it."

"Me?" Mitchell asked, astounded at the idea.

"You showed real sand, gettin' out of all them scrapes. A new station needs someone with their wits about them. Be a rise in pay for you too. Besides, it'll keep you out of Salt Lake for a good while. I do not know what the law'll do now they're all riled up over Winston. I even tried talkin' peaceably with Esmeralda but she's havin' none of it."

"I dunno, Don. I've only just got used to bein' a rider."

"Well, sure! You can still be a rider. No problem there. Just take a few months to get the new station established. Let the dust settle for once."

Mitchell blew out his cheeks, unsure of what to say.

"I'll tell you what," Don said. "Sleep on it. Hunker down in your bunk for a while. Just don't go wanderin' around town. They're liable to think you're a ghost."

Mitchell stood up.

"Thanks, Don. I reckon I could do with a bit of a think about this one."

"You do that. Oh, one more thing," Don said. He patted his pockets, retrieving a letter. Mitchell recognized the handwriting straight away. "This came for you yesterday. I was worried I'd have to open it and write back about how you was deceased."

Mitchell took the letter. It suddenly struck him how lucky he was. He sat down quickly, hand shaking a little as he held Isabelle's letter.

"You take your time," Don said. "Read what your sweetheart wrote there and think on it real good."

Chapter Six
Egan Station

*D*ear Mitchell,

    It was wonderful to get your letter and hear all your news. Goodness, what adventures! Ma was very impressed to have it delivered by Pony Express and to hear of your success there. It raised her spirits no end. Truth is, I have some terrible news to tell you. Mitchell, my Pa passed away a few weeks after you lit out. He went to bed that night, same as always, but when Ma tried to rouse him next morning, he was gone. I can't tell you how upset we've been since. I know you didn't always see eye-to-eye with Pa, but I told him my heart was yours and he accepted that.

    After the funeral we found out that there was some money owing to the bank. Now, Ma and I are working as hard as we can at the store to pay it off. You know the bank manager, Fred Whittaker? He's a slippery customer and comes by every so often with ledger books and going on and on about "principal" and "interest" until I could run off crying with frustration. I'm stubborn though, as you know, and I won't let him bully us. Truth be told, I think he wants me to marry his fishy character of a son. Keeps bringing him by as an "associate manager" and telling my mother how good his prospects at the bank are. I've had other suitors too, hanging around the place like flies.

I wish you were here, Mitchell, to help us put things back to rights. I know you wanted to take off for a spell and see the world, and Pa didn't make it easy for us to be together. But Pa, God rest his soul, has passed on now and we are struggling. I know you've always had a tough time settling on one thing and that's why I think it's swell you have settled on the Pony Express. Is it very dangerous, though? I was a little shocked to read about you having to shoot your gun. I hope it was only to scare off a rattlesnake or some other critter.

At first I didn't believe that letter was from you because it was written in such a fancy style. I guess you have been keeping your writing skill hidden from me all this time. Maybe you had a little help on it? You don't have to impress me with fancy words, Mitchell Stone. Like I told Pa, you have my heart and always will. Simple and straight. You be careful of yourself out there beyond the mountains and come back as soon as you can. Ma and I are holding on as best we can, but it's tough sometimes.

Your Isabelle

***

Mitchell leaned back in his bunk, Isabelle's letter on his chest. He had read it about five times now and still could not decide what to do. Part of him wanted to take the money he had saved and get on the fastest pony back to Wichita. He remembered Earl Whittaker, the bank manager's son. There was always something odd about him. Once, a few of the kids had gone fishing and Earl had caught a small fry. Instead of throwing it back, he had kept whacking its head against a rock. Mitchell hadn't liked the cruel gleam in Earl's eye.

Who knew what other varmints like Earl Whittaker were sniffing around the General Store, looking to seize an opportunity? The thought of it made Mitchell's blood boil. He thought better of Isabelle, though. He should have known she would see through his having Don write that letter. She was tougher than he gave her credit for and wouldn't easily have her head turned. They had promised to each other, and they meant it. However, it sounded like the business might be struggling, so every penny he made out here would only help when he finally returned. And now Don was offering him more money as a manager…

Mitchell kicked the wall in frustration. Whenever he could not make up his mind, he bucked like a skittish colt. He stood up and put his belt on. Tucking the letter into his pocket, he made for the door. He needed to get out and clear his head.

"Where d'you think you're goin'?" Don asked as Mitchell strode past.

"I gotta get outa here for a bit."

"I told you. If anybody recognizes you, there might be trouble."

"Look Don, I'm goin' stir crazy in there. Why don't you lend me that big old Stetson you never use? I'll keep it low over my eyes."

"Hmm. Oh, alright," Don said, retrieving the hat and tossing it to Mitchell. "Jus' be careful. An' stick to the outskirts of town. When you come back, I want you to decide. Let me know if you'll take the commission at Egan Station. I got one or two more I could ask."

"All right, Don," Mitchell said, fixing the hat down low over his eyes as he departed from the office.

Outside, the day was overcast. A high canopy of clouds covered the sky like curdled cream. Mitchell instantly felt ridiculous wearing the hat so low and pushed it back from his face. He strode out of the yard, preoccupied with his troubles. The streets were as busy as ever, although Mitchell hardly noticed. Mitchell had intended to keep away from the main streets but, in his distracted state, wandered through the main part of town.

"Mitchell Stone! As I live and breathe. You seem to have nine lives..."

Mitchell looked up. He didn't recognize her at first. She was wearing a respectable dress of deep crimson crushed velvet, buttoned up to her neck. Her curls were tamed beneath a matching hat. It was her arched eyebrows and piercing green eyes that caught his attention.

"Esmeralda!" Mitchell exclaimed. "Sorry. I didn't recognize you."

"Few do when I'm not at work. I'm just back from the bank. Won't you join me for a... cup of tea?"

Her gaze drifted to the fine hotel they were outside. Mitchell hadn't even noticed it.

"Certainly. That's if...you know...Mr. Winston doesn't mind."

"Tobias? Hmm. He's in no position to object to what I do these days..."

She swept by him, walking forward a couple of paces. She turned back and inclined her head.

"Well?" she asked. "Are you coming?"

Mitchell removed his hat. So much for the disguise.

"All right, Ma'am. Not sure if'n I've ever had tea before."

Esmeralda chuckled, flashing him a lop-sided smile.

"You never know," she said. "You might even like it."

He followed her through the large glass doors. The hotel lobby was cool and well-appointed.

"Miss Gosling!" declared a man from behind a large desk. "So lovely to see you."

"Thank you so much, Chester."

"Will you be taking lunch with us this afternoon," Chester enquired, hurrying over to them.

"Ah, no. A bit early, I think. Just tea."

"Very good. Come this way."

The maitre'd somehow ignored Mitchell entirely, yet expertly guide him into the restaurant. Inside, the polished tables were mostly devoid of customers. Chester seated them in a discreet corner, promising to return with tea. Esmeralda smiled happily.

"I do like it here. What they charge is outrageous, but I suppose that's the secret to a successful business."

Mitchell slowly shook his head.

"I didn't know you was so..."

"Respectable? Oh, you'd be surprised what the most respectable people really do. I run into many of my biggest customers in this hotel."

She cocked her head to one side. It impressed Mitchell how elegant she could look.

"Let me start by saying I'm very annoyed with the Pony Express these days. You boys have been shooting up The Golden Lily far too many times. Now. Tell me where you've been."

She rested one hand under her chin, listening with a rapt expression as Mitchell recounted his adventures. He only paused when Chester came with a tray laden with teacups and small pastries. Esmeralda waved the man away, staring at Mitchell until he continued.

"My goodness!" she said, when he reached the part about returning to Salt Lake. "You really are quite the hero. Those Paiute are a real menace. Utah will get nowhere while they are allowed to roam free. How's your tea? You've hardly touched it!"

"It ain't as strong as coffee, is it? Bit bitter too."

"Well, it helps if you add milk and sugar. Go ahead..."

Mitchell did as instructed. Esmeralda toyed with her own half-empty cup.

"I'm so glad I ran into you," she said. "I must confess that I find you very... interesting. Ever since I first laid eyes on you with Tobias."

She put down her cup and reached forward, taking Mitchell's hand. Mitchell looked up in surprise.

"Ma'am?"

"Yes. Tobias, Mr. Winston, is only a front. I own the deed to The Golden Lily. He has been useful. A woman alone can't do business in this town, and he's helped me where I've got today."

It amazed Mitchell how cool her touch was, like a spring breeze.

"But I'm tired of his antics. Lately, he's been gambling too much and getting in too many fights. And now he's gone and got himself shot, making a mess all over my establishment. Ugh. Typical man. No offence..."

She gave Mitchell an arched smile. He gulped and nodded.

"So I have a proposal. A man like you can do so much better than chasing around, being attacked by bandits and Indians. All you have to do is come back to The Golden Lily tonight. I'll let you in the back way. Slip upstairs to his room. He's lying there feeling sorry for himself all day long. Then just... Well, you get the idea."

"You want me to—"

She leaned forward and kissed him. Mitchell stared at her in amazement. She opened her eyes and looked back.

"Oh, say nothing," she said, a finger to his lips. "I know what you want to do. Tobias has tried to kill you twice now. Fate has put you back into my world. A hero like you can save me from all the cruel things he's done to me and some of my girls..."

Mitchell moistened his lips. He still could feel the softness of her kiss.

"That's... That's terrible, Esmeralda. I'm right flattered you think so highly of me. But... Why have you put up with it? Why don't you get rid of him yourself?"

"Oh!" Her features grew cross, a thundercloud across the sun. "He's turned out more devious than ever, I thought. Never lets that little peashooter out of his hand. Needs a man to finish him off. Besides, I don't trust how he's so well in with the law. Suspicion would turn to me and they wouldn't think twice about hanging a woman around here, especially one like me."

She gave him another coy look. Mitchell sat with his mouth open, unsure what to say. She laughed pleasantly, taking both his hands.

"This is so wonderful! You come by after midnight. I'll be waiting by the back door and show you upstairs. Oh, the shock when he sees you. I wish I could be there to witness it. Afterwards, well…"

She leaned forward and kissed Mitchell again. There was an urgency to her action this time. Mitchell blushed at the experience. Esmeralda chortled with delight.

"Oh Mitchell," she said. "I need a man like you to help me run the place. You and I. There's no telling what we couldn't achieve."

It took Mitchell nearly half a minute to compose himself.

"That's… That's some plan you have, Esmeralda. I'm mighty obliged to you for… for everything. I just… I just got to go back to the station and settle up a few things."

He stood up. Esmeralda stood as well. She stuck out her hand.

"Good. I'll expect you later. I feel this is the beginning of a beautiful partnership."

"Thank you, Ma'am," Mitchell said awkwardly. He shook her hand. "It sure is."

He grabbed his hat and backed out of the dining room, tea only half-finished. Chester gave him a venomous look as he stumbled back out onto the street. Mitchell's head was reeling at the possibilities as he made his way back to the station. This time he kept his hat low and watched whoever he encountered. He hurried into the office, but Don wasn't there. He made his way back to the kitchen where Don was spooning down Watkin's latest fare. Don looked up, his eyes questioning.

"I'd like to accept your offer, Don. I'm in more trouble in this town than I ever thought."

***

They were up early the next day as they had to spend some time making a rope corral for a few horses to bring with them on the trail. The sun was clearing the wall of the station yard as they readied to leave. Mitchell slung his saddlebag containing his few belongings over the side of his horse. He raised himself up into the saddle. Hellfire snorted and stamped his feet, eager to be on the road. Don was reluctant to let him take the fiery horse at first, but Mitchell had his way.

"We ain't goin' to be bringing any mail," Don had said. "'Cause we gotta take these horses along. So no hijinks, racin' around. Hellfire won't like it."

"He'll behave," Mitchell said, patting the half-mustang's neck. "We have an understandin'."

Don saddled his pony and led them out of the station. Mitchell looked back over his shoulder, giving the place a wistful look. He wasn't sure why, but he felt he would never return. He shrugged and looked ahead, hauling on Hellfire's reins to keep him from bolting forward. The town was quiet, and they were on the road south with little fuss. The pace was moderate, to keep the riderless horses from straying too far.

"What made up your mind?" asked Don, pulling his horse alongside Mitchell's once the road was quiet.

"Had a little run-in with Esmeralda yesterday..." Mitchell paused, unsure of what to say next.

"Ha hah, Say no more." Don said. "She's somethin', ain't she? I reckon she'll be married to the Mayor one of these days. What did she say to you?"

Mitchell shook his head.

"I couldn't figure out if she wanted to marry me... or trap me and have me shot."

"She might've been figurin' to do both. Yep, she's the real brains of that operation all right."

Mitchell focused on the road ahead, making no reply.

"What about your sweetheart back home? She like my honey words? You goin' to write to her about Esmeralda?"

Mitchell ignored Don's last jibe.

"Isabelle's Pa died. She wants me to come back. Help with the store."

"That so?"

Don said no more. Mitchell glanced over at him.

"She said the bank manager's after them," Mitchell said.

"Hmm. That's tough, all right. Yet here you are, headin' away from them."

"I know it," said Mitchell. "It was a tough choice to make. But I figure If I go back there now, it's goin' to be more hard graft, scramblin' to make ends meet." Mitchell sighed. "I'm goin' to make a go of this station. Maybe after a year, I'll go back home with a big passel of money saved. Send that bank manager runnin' and marry Isabelle proper. She's strong. She'll hang on until I do."

"That's a mighty fine plan," Don said. "Just hope you can stick it out."

"What're you sayin'? I said I mean to."

Don nodded a few times, staring off to the mountains across the plain. He was chewing on a little tobacco for distraction. Mitchell watched his jaw grind up and down.

"Don?" he asked, when no further response was forthcoming.

"What? Oh. That's a fine plan alright. Just don't be too surprised if things change. I was married once, you know. Good while back. I left her behind to come get the gold they said was just floating about in the rivers out here. I meant to go back home with it, too. Just found none of that gold. Then some time passed, and I was too ashamed to go back."

"You still could," Mitchell said, although his voice sounded unsure.

"Yeah. Who knows? Could be she's still waitin' for me. Like she said she would. Seems to me like all women are the same, though. Just like Esmeralda there. In the end, after all the talk of love, it comes down to money and they change their hearts quick."

Mitchell said nothing. He stared down the trail.

"Listen," Don said, after a long pause. "Just don't be surprised if the years go by and you're still out here runnin' about on ponies." He gave a quick laugh. "It ain't such a terrible life either. But if you really mean to, you stick to that plan. Keep writin' to Isabelle and savin' your money. I can help you pen another letter, if you like."

"Ah, thanks Don. I appreciate that, but she's already wise to us. I mean to write myself this time."

"Huh. Well, it sounds like you got a smart cookie there. Mebbe you two will make a go of it after all."

He lapsed into silence. They didn't speak again for many miles. Occasionally, one pony would try to wander and Mitchell would head back to keep it in line. Hellfire was despondent at the slow pace and Mitchell shared the mood. The sun beat down on them as the day wore on. After noon, they came to a thin creek.

"How's about we stop here for a spell?" Don said, slowing his mount. "Water these horses."

Mitchell's only reply was to halt Hellfire. He came down off the saddle and led the pony over the water. Soon they lined all the ponies up along the stream, heads down in the water. Mitchell and Don sat on a rock, chewing on biscuits from their saddlebags.

"What is that?" Mitchell asked.

A low rumbling came from all about. Perhaps it had been there for a while but was only now properly audible.

"Shoot!" Don said, standing up and scanning the horizon. "That's a big herd."

He pointed north to a rapidly expanding cloud of dust.

"What the...?" asked Mitchell. He had to raise his voice against the thundering noise. Suddenly, the surrounding ground shook and trembled.

"Buffalo," Don shouted. "Grab the horses. Stay in the water."

Mitchell and Don scrambled about. The other horses were spooked and resisted their efforts. Only Hellfire was calm and helped lead the other horses into the middle of the stream.

"Are we safe here?" yelled Mitchell.

"You got your gun ready?" Don yelled back.

Mitchell gulped and reached for his pistol. He noticed Don had none.

Ahead of them, the cloud of dust resolved to individual bison. Their massive heads were low, and they ran as if death itself was chasing them. Mitchell put his fear to one side and trained his gun on the approaching beasts. He couldn't help but feel a thrill at the sight of so many of them racing forward with a singular purpose. Don yelled something else, but it was impossible to hear.

A great phalanx of buffalo rushed by. Whatever instinct dictating the herd's behavior stopped them from crossing into the stream. Don and Mitchell held on as tight as they could while the horses bucked and kicked. Eventually, it proved too much, and they broke away, running off in the opposite direction from the relentlessly driving beasts. The ground shook as if an immense angry child was slamming it again and again. After just five minutes, the bulk of them had passed. Finally, it was just stragglers and buffalo calves trotting after the quickly receding mass.

"Damn!" said Don when he could be heard again. "Goin' to take some time to get our horses back."

"That happen often?" Mitchell asked, holstering his gun.

"Just this time of year. We got lucky, I suppose. We could've been ridin' when they came on us. I should've thought to hobble the horses."

"Look!" Mitchell said.

He pointed to a lone horse about a hundred yards distant.

"I reckon that's Hellfire. He ain't afraid of no buffalo."

Mitchell took off, sprinting towards his horse.

"Come back!" shouted Don. Mitchell hardly heard him.

Don shook his head and sat down on the rock again, pondering what to do next.

Mitchell's heart was thundering in his chest when he reached the horse.

"Well done, Hellfire. You weren't afraid, were you?"

It took a little coaxing and the horse shying away once or twice, but Mitchell got a hand on the saddle horn and hauled himself up.

"Let's see where the others are."

He urged the half-mustang forward. Soon they were galloping over the plain. Mitchell was fearing he should have returned to Don when he spotted the other horses. They were running about in frightened circles in the brush.

"Whoa, Hellfire! Let's not spook them anymore than they already are."

He slowed his pony to a walk. The others spotted them and slowed. Hellfire snorted and surged forward. To Mitchell's surprise, the ponies stood still, waiting obediently.

"I guess you're the chief of this here tribe!" Mitchell said.

He jumped off and grabbed the ropes hanging loose to the horses. Don's horse only had reins, and it took Mitchell a while to corner him. In the end, Hellfire came forward and butted his head against the recalcitrant pony. The other animal immediately stopped its fractious behavior, bowing its head to let Mitchell grab the reins.

"Well, Hellfire, I can't thank you enough," Mitchell said, tying all the ponies into a single train to lead back to Don.

Mitchell paused, scanning the horizon in confusion. Which way had he come? A sinking feeling came over him.

"Blast you, Mitchell Stone," he rebuked himself. "You're always running off without thinking things through. Now how'm I goin' to find my way back to Don?"

He sat down in the dirt, anger and fear warring within him. The risk was he might strike off and go completely wide of the mark, leaving Don out there. As he sat on the ground, cursing his lot, he spotted Hellfire give a snort and start walking forward; the other horses following.

"You know the way! Of course you do."

Mitchell got up and ran after his horse. Hellfire stamped and shook his blond mane when he approached.

"Alright!" Mitchell said, backing off. "I won't ride you. You lead us back to Don. I'll bet he'll be some glad to see us when we return."

It took a couple of hours to find the stream again. When they did, the sun was setting amidst a rosette of pink and orange clouds. There was no sign of Don.

"Well, Hellfire. I reckon you earned a drink, anyway. I can't tell if this was the exact spot where we left Don."

He let the ponies drink, pondering what to do next. If it got much darker, there was no way he could find Don. He cupped his hands around his mouth.

"Hallo!" he called. "Don? You out here? Where the blazes are you?"

It was silent for a long while before Don popped up from behind a rock.

"Howdy," Don said with a smirk. "You took your sweet time."

***

They camped that night by the river after hobbling the ponies. They debated whether the animals even needed to be restrained, they were so obviously weary after the events of the day. In the end, the risk of another buffalo stampede was enough. Mitchell's sleep was fitful, and he tossed and turned on his thin bedroll. It wasn't the hard ground that kept him awake, he was used to that; it was the thought of Isabelle and the bank manager's son that haunted him.

"Best make a start," Don called to him early the next morning.

"Don't feel like I slept at all," Mitchell said with a groan, rolling over to watch Don putting together a campfire.

"I'll fix some coffee and you'll be fine. We still got a way to go until Egan Canyon."

The coffee, when it was ready, helped. Before the sun was over the mountains, they had the horses ready and found their way back onto the trail. Mitchell dozed occasionally. At one point, Don asked him something, and he jerked awake.

"You sleepin' in the saddle?" Don said. "You really are Pony Express!"

They continued on that way for most of the rest of the day. By afternoon, Mitchell noticed they were closing on a series of hills covered with short scrubby trees.

"Yonder's the mouth of Egan Canyon. Station's about half an hour in."

Mitchell rode Hellfire up to Don. He looked in the direction Don was pointing.

"What trees are those?" he asked.

"Mostly serviceberry. That's what they call 'em. Prickly things. They'll rip a horse to shreds if you run through them too fast. Berries ain't fit for eatin' neither. C'mon. Let's try to make the station before sundown."

Mitchell gave one more look at the hills before returning Hellfire to the rear of the little herd of horses, urging them forward.

They made good time to the mouth of the canyon. The stunted trees rose thick on the steep hills about them and the trail was broken, switching back and forth every twenty yards. It took longer than Don's promised half an hour to reach their destination. Mitchell was despairing Don had mistaken the way when they turned a corner that opened onto a slight clearing. A low adobe building with a log roof was nestled against the steep canyon walls. A small barn and horse enclosure alongside were the only other addition to the isolated station.

"Here we are," Don said.

"Pretty small, ain't it?" Mitchell replied. "It don't even have a proper sign saying Pony Express or anything."

"Never mind about that. Few lookin' to read a sign out here."

Mitchell's heart sank at the thought of being stuck out here. He looked about the darkening valley. An eerie quiet had descended on the steep hillsides.

"Is it always this quiet?" asked Mitchell.

"What were you expectin'," said Don, chuckling, "San Francisco? Now, where's Frank?"

Don trotted his horse forward the last thirty yards, leaving Mitchell to tend to the tired horses. With a frown,

Mitchell busied himself with the animals. He herded them into the enclosure and made sure there was water and feed for them. Pinpricks of stars were coming out when he stepped into the little station.

"There he is," Frank called, looking up with a broad smile on his face. He beckoned Mitchell to the plain table. He had prepared a simple meal of pork and cornmeal. "Here. Help yourself to some food. Don's been filling me in on your adventures! You know, we was sure you were a goner. Figured it was that snake Winston. Me and Jonah put paid to him—"

"Yes," interrupted Don. "That's why I had to station you here."

"I'm much obliged you stood up for me, Frank." Mitchell said. "Guess we had to come out here to thank you."

"I sure am glad you came. I don't take much to bein' here on my own."

"Hmph," grunted Don. "Even though Mitchell started at the Express after you, he's showed he has what it takes to run a place like this. You alright with that, Frank?"

Frank laughed a little.

"Alright?" Frank said. "Relieved is what I am! Lookin' forward to when I can hit the road again."

"Well, you just keep this station as your base," Don said. "Make sure you keep going down-trail too. No goin' back up to Salt Lake City for a good while."

"Yes, Don."

Frank hung his head. He reminded Mitchell of a penitent schoolboy.

"So," said Mitchell, pushing away his empty plate. "What have we got to do around here?"

Don leaned back on his chair.

"There's looking after the ponies, mainly," he said. "Plus the supply wagon comes by every week. You got to check it and enter everything into the ledger. Then there's waitin' for the riders. You got to have a mount ready for 'em at a moment's notice."

"We can take turns!" Frank said, brightening.

"Yes," agreed Don. "It's a good idea to break it into shifts."

"All right," Mitchell said. "Feels a bit like a lighthouse keeper…"

"I' God!" Don exclaimed. "You couldn't find yourself further from the ocean. Where'd you get that idea?"

"Oh, a picture my mother used to have on the mantle. It had a lighthouse on a cliff overlooking the sea."

"I suppose you could think of it along those lines," mused Don. "You put out the light when the riders need it."

"Plus," added Frank. "You got pirates to watch out for—"

"Pirates!" Mitchell asked. "What're you talkin' about?"

"Oh, not really pirates, I s'pose. There's been talk about bandits attackin' some stations hereabouts…"

"Where'd you hear that?" Don asked.

"Ralph, the old timer that was keepin' the place before me. Said they raided him six months ago. They couldn't take much. Before we set it up as a station proper…"

"Hmm," Don said. "First, I heard of it. It's true, though. There have been attacks on stations. You got to make a point of not keepin' any money around. Make sure you always got a firearm handy, unlike when you're ridin'."

"Then there are your friends, the Paiutes," Frank added.

"What?" Mitchell asked, alarmed.

"All right," Don said, standing up. "You boys don't want to be dwelling too much on all of that. How's about we have a game of cards?"

Mitchell and Frank look at each other.

"But what about the oath?"

"That danged oath don't apply so much out here. Besides, you boys will be shootin' at shadows if you don't take your minds off things."

He went over to the wall where the saddlebags were hanging from hooks. He produced a well worn deck of cards.

"I'm happy to donate these to you boys. Something to keep things a little interesting around here. Provided you let me win back some of that fat paycheck I'm dishin' out every month."

Mitchell and Frank grinned at him. They cleared off the plates and settled into playing cards. Frank had no money to gamble and had to get a stake from Don. They played a little pinochle, but Don clearly had the upper hand. Frank insisted they switch to Faro as he had done alright playing it at The Emerald Isle. After an hour, Frank was cleaned out again. Mitchell was a conservative player but was steadily losing as well.

"Say!" Frank exclaimed. "What was all that you told us about not gamblin', Don? You done cleaned us out in no time!"

"Ha ha!" Don said, moving his chewing tobacco around in his mouth. "I ain't always been in the Pony Express. When I was up in the Sierra Nevadas prospectin', we used to do a lot of gamblin'. The only gold in them mountains was at the card table. I'll tell you boys what, why don't you practice while I'm gone? I'm off tomorrow morning and won't be back for a month. In the meantime, you both can pass the time learning how to play proper. I feel bad takin' you to the cleaners so much, Frank."

"Oh, thank you very much," Frank said. "Proper good Samaritan you are, Don."

"Wait," said Mitchell, ignoring their banter. "Did you say you were goin' tomorrow?"

"That's right," Don said, shuffling the cards expertly. "Got to get back to Salt Lake City. Make sure everything keeps running smoothly."

"Um," Mitchell said. "I got to give you a letter. To take back to Isabelle."

Don and Frank exchanged smirks.

"I'll wipe your slate clean," Don said. "If'n you read it out to us."

Mitchell stood up, took his bag off the peg and headed back to the little bedroom he was to share with Frank.

"Mebbe not," Mitchell said. "Besides, I got to write it first."

Chapter Seven
Longing for Home

*D*ear Isabelle,

I was sorry to hear the news about your Pa. He was a good man and I reckon we could have patched things up. He just wanted to keep you safe. It's too bad he didn't see that was what I wanted too. Your poor Ma must be in a bad way. It can't be good to have men like Whittaker and his son pestering her. It's a good thing you're there to help. When I got your letter first, I nearly got right on the fastest pony here and headed straight back to Kansas. I have missed you that much, Isabelle. When I thought of your loss and how tough it must be for you. Well, I was nearly in the saddle and right on the road...

Then I talked to Don, he's the manager of the station in Salt Lake. He's also the man who got me the job in the Pony Express. Truth be told, Don helped me write that last letter to you. I'm right sorry about that, Isabelle. It won't happen again. I used to find it awful hard to settle to writing or anything like that, but I've changed since starting work here.

Anyway, Don and I had a good talk. He says if I hold out on the job here for a few months, I can head back to you with a princely sum of money. He's even promoted me to manager of my own station, which means I get half again what I'm on already. If I save up enough, I can use the money to set us up proper when I get back. You tell your Ma that is what I aim to do.

The station I'm in charge of is in the middle of Egan Canyon. It's a couple of days' ride out from Salt Lake. The scenery is right pretty here, with lots of short trees all covered with berries right now. I can take a walk right up the steep hill and see out across the plains. I wish I could show you, Isabelle! If you like, maybe we can talk about settling out here later on? Depending on how things are with your mother, of course.

It is still wild out here. I've met the Paiute people now. They are an interesting bunch. Although they don't seem to do so well these days. I've heard there are some bandits around, but I have not seen any. It seems to me that the place is too quiet for bandits. That's what I like out here— the quiet. It has settled me, living out in the wide open plains with only my horse for company. Well, that's not entirely true. I have Frank here with me at the station. He is a fine fellow, although not very good at cards. Don't worry, we don't play for serious money like some other riders. We play just to pass the time. And I guess it's not always quiet, I had a run-in with a stampeding herd of buffalo on the way here. That was some sight, I can tell you!

I should finish up now. Don is heading back to Salt Lake City today, and I said I would write to you before he left. If you want me back, just you write to me, and straight away I will come. Like I said, I wanted to, but then I thought of how strong you are. If you can just hang on for a few months, then I will have a little fortune saved for us and can set things right when I return. You are ever in my heart, Isabelle. Those are my own words, and I mean them faithfully.

Mitchell

% Pony Express Egan Station,
Egan Canyon,
Utah Territory

***

After a few days, Mitchell and Frank settled into a routine. They split the night into shifts, so either of them would be awake in case another rider should approach. The first time Mitchell heard the approaching bugle echoing around the steep hills, he thought the End of Days had arrived. Even though it was Frank's shift, Mitchell joined him, preparing a fresh horse in the dark.

"Don't know if we need shifts, Frank. Not if the bugle's that loud."

"Maybe you don't but I sleep like the dead. Besides, what if they lose their bugle or something?"

Mitchell had no time to reply as the rider pulled up and swung off his horse.

After that first night, he learned to sleep through the bugling when not his turn. Frank certainly had no problem ignoring the clarion while sleeping.

At the end of the first week, they had their first visit from the supply cart. The large two-horse covered wagon was laden down with feed for animals and people, spare clothes, bedding, and any other necessaries. A partner who kept a rifle ready accompanied the rider. He didn't come down from the seat to help unload, but remained on the buckboard, vigilantly scanning the hills.

"You troubled by bandits much?" Mitchell asked the man, who had introduced himself as Stanley.

"Can't be too careful," Stanley replied. "We are a temptin' target for all kinds out here."

He dropped the last sack by their station entrance.

"That should be enough to keep you goin' for the next week," Stanley said. "You got it all entered in the ledger book?"

Mitchell showed him the book.

"Good. I'll just sign off on the bottom."

The man took Mitchell's quill and scrawled his signature at the bottom of the row of figures.

"How much further you got to go?" Mitchell asked.

"Let's see… It'll take a day or so 'til we reach Fort Laramie. I reckon we'll be doin' well to get there by tomorrow. We'll stop there for a spell and turn around."

"Fort Laramie? Do you know if Lieutenant Weed is stationed there?"

"Could be," Stanley said, scratching his chin. "Mebbe I heard there was a new Lieutenant coming. I have little to do with the military. 'Cept when we run into trouble. They're the only law out here. Them and Jim up there."

Stanley nodded over to Jim sitting up on the wagon. Jim tipped his cap in reply.

"We best be moving on," Stanley said. "You want anything for us to bring back next time?"

"No, don't think so," Mitchell replied. "Fred inside is taking his shift now. I thought I might grab a rifle and do a bit of hunting. Catch some rabbit or deer. No offence to the food you bring us, but..."

"None taken!" Stanley said with a grin.

"I don't fancy huntin' here in the deepest spot of the canyon. Maybe I could hitch a ride out a way yonder? I could make my way back on foot."

"I don't mind," Stanley said, "So long as you don't mind riding in the wagon. No room up front for another."

"That sounds fine," Mitchell said. "I'll get my rifle and tell Frank."

Frank made no objection to Mitchell's rushed explanation. Within a few minutes, Mitchell was hunkered down under the covered canvas, rifle in hand and surrounded with supplies. He heard Stanley's "hee-yah" and the wagon lurch forward. Mitchell settled himself against a sack of grain and closed his eyes. He didn't mean to but soon drifted into a light doze, the rhythmic sway of the wagon lulling him to sleep. Mitchell had a brief dream of racing along the plains atop Hellfire, trying to escape something but couldn't see what it was.

BANG!

The ring of gunshot woke him instantly. The wagon shook as the horses panicked and bucked. Mitchell heard a heavy thump from up front.

"What's goin' on?" he hissed.

"It's Jim!" called Stanley. "They got him. You stay low. Looks like there's about three—"

Another shot stopped Stanley's words. The wagon rattled forward at an awkward pitch. Mitchell kept low, rifle ready. He could only see the trail behind him, two riders galloping into view. It took all his nerve to stay put. His only chance was to surprise them when they halted the wagon.

After a hair-raising ride, the spooked horses slowed. He heard the riders shouting to each other as they drew alongside. With a thud, one of them jumped from his horse onto the buckboard. Mitchell could see the top of his head through a slit in the canvas. Some more yelling and he had the wagon halted. Mitchell held his breath and waited.

"You got 'em under control, Earl?"

The second rider flashed by Mitchell's view as he drew his horse up to the front of the wagon. Mitchell heard a low groan of pain.

"Yessir," replied Earl. "Looks like this old-timer's still got some life left in him."

"That so?" the other man said. His voice was flat and without emotion. "Better do something 'bout that…"

This time the gunshot was so close, Mitchell could smell the powder. He listened as Stanley's body was dumped from the wagon. He ground his teeth together. They just killed an injured man in cold blood! It was all he could do not to dash out screaming.

"Damn, Pete! Didn't have to kill him right there, did you?"

"It needed doing," came Pete's reply. "I'm going to check the wagon. See nothing got too damaged."

Mitchell waited with his rifle ready, but it wasn't cocked. He would have to be quick as he heard the bandit come down from his horse and walk around the wagon. His head appeared and Mitchell's rifle clicked as he readied it. Pete ducked at the sound, but Mitchell was ready. He stood and leaned out of the wagon, firing at the man scrambling down the back.

"Hey!" called Earl. "What's goin' on back—"

He didn't get to finish his sentence. Mitchell turned and dashed as far forward in the wagon as he could. He snapped the lever, ejecting the shell, and pointed the barrel out through the canvas.

"Don't move!" Mitchell growled. "Raise your hands where I can see 'em."

"Dang!" said Earl, complying. "Did you just finish off Pete?"

"Shut up!" Mitchell said. "Keep those hands up."

It was tricky crawling out over the supplies to sit beside Earl, all the while keeping a gun pointed at him. Luckily for Mitchell, some cargo had tumbled forward when the horses bolted. He positioned himself alongside Earl who sat, ashen-faced, his hands in the air.

"I will shoot if you try anything," Mitchell said. "How many more of you are there?"

"Why, there ain't but me an' Pete. An' I reckon you done finished him."

"That so?" Mitchell said. He glanced quickly at Stanley's body slumped on the ground. "Stanley called out three. Before you plugged him."

"Might be the old man was seein' things."

Mitchell didn't like the look of Earl's weak smile. Earl was a sorry sight: his breeches were torn and dusty like the rest of his clothes.

"Get off this wagon. Lie on the dirt. Face down."

With more deferential smiling, Earl shuffled off the wagon and laid on the ground. Mitchell leaped off and picked up a loop of loose rope from the wagon's side. Without a word, he tied Earl's hands behind his back. He noticed the man was missing his right index finger. Earl kept talking, face in the dirt.

"What you fixin' to do with me? You know, there's a lot of good stuff in the back of that wagon. We could halve it—"

A crack of gunfire split the air. Mitchell felt the whoosh of the bullet as it missed him and hit Earl. Earl howled in pain, the bullet clipping his left shoulder. Mitchell jumped down to the other side of the wagon and crouched behind a wheel.

"Nobody else with you, huh?" he said to Earl.

"That crazy Indian," Earl howled through gritted teeth. "We told him to hang back in case things got tough."

"Indian?"

"Pete got him as a guide. They know the country best out here. Never trusted him myself. Ow!"

Earl squirmed with pain.

"Can you call him off? I'll see to your wound if you do."

Earl lay still for a while. Mitchell was wondering if he had expired.

"Hey, John!" he yelled out. "You get out of here. Go get more! Like we—"

Mitchell used the butt of the rifle to crack Earl on the back of his head. Earl lay still, unconscious.

"That was stupid," Mitchell muttered.

He crouched as close to the wagon as he could, straining his ears at the silence. Five minutes passed. Finally, he dared stand and peer over to the hill where he thought the shooter might be. On the horizon, he spotted a solitary rider. Although Mitchell could see he wore regular clothes, something about the way he sat on his horse convinced Mitchell he was Paiute. Mitchell stared up at him along the barrel of his rifle.

"You come down here and we can work something out," he called.

The figure on the hill didn't move.

"This is a regular stand-off," Mitchell said aloud. "Doubt I could hit him up on the hill."

After a tense few minutes, the man called back.

"Stay there!"

He turned his horse about and galloped away.

Mitchell put down his rifle.

"If you think I'm stayin' put, you got another think comin'."

He went to Earl, sprawled on the ground. The man's shoulder was clipped, but it was only a flesh wound. There was a small trickle of blood around his hairline from Mitchell's rifle butt. Mitchell dived into the wagon. He couldn't find bandages, but there was a loose shirt. He ripped a strip off, returning to staunch Earl's wounds with it. Then he pulled the fabric in a tourniquet around the man's arm. Earl moaned, but his eyes remained shut.

"All right, Earl," Mitchell said, "into the wagon you go."

He hoisted the man up. It was awkward at first as Earl's hands were tied and he was out cold. However, the man was scrawny and once Mitchell got him up, he could lift him to the back of the wagon. With a grunt, Mitchell dumped Earl into the back. Earl muttered something incoherent.

"I reckon you won't be able to give me much trouble trussed up back there."

Mitchell hurried back to the front of the wagon and saw to the horses. They were calm now. Mitchell wondered at this. How often was this wagon attacked by bandits? He scratched the back of his head, pondering what he should do next. He could never outrun men on horseback with a loaded wagon so he gathered up the guns placing them at the ready behind the box-seat. Mitchell looked down at the three bodies of Stanley, Jim and Pete. It was a gruesome sight.

"I don't got time to bury you boys," Mitchell said. "That John guy could be back with a posse any minute. I figure there's no point in heading back to Frank at the station. They'll only catch me. Best bet is to head for the fort."

He rummaged around the wagon seat, finding a map. He let out a relieved sigh. The Pony Express always equipped their riders well. Studying the map, he made a rough reckoning of his location. He noticed the trail looped south for a long while to another station before heading west to Fort Laramie.

"I can't outrun them, so here's hoping they don't expect me to cut west," he muttered, folding away the map.

He snapped the reins, directing the horses forward. Although the trail wasn't much out here, Mitchell didn't dare veer off it. Every few minutes, the wagon lurched at some hollow or hillock of the rough terrain, and Mitchell was sure he would hear a wheel or axle crack. Yet he had to urge on the horses to go as fast as possible. The animals didn't like it and stopped occasionally in confusion.

"C'mon!" he shouted, desperation getting the better of him. "Who knows who's on our trail!"

He pulled on the reins, halting the wagon. An idea came to him. He pulled a small hatchet from the wagon's running board and jumped down. There was a small cluster of serviceberry trees nearby. He hacked them down hastily, returning to the wagon. Looking in on Earl, he pulled on the rope looped around him.

"Wha?" mumbled Earl groggily.

"Never you mind," Mitchell said. "I'm makin' sure your friends don't follow our tracks."

He chopped off a couple of lengths of rope and secured the bushes behind the wheels. It wasn't perfect, but it might do in the fading light. Mitchell jumped back on the driver seat and got the horses moving. He didn't push them as hard now, instead taking as zig-zagging a route as he dared. He hoped that whoever John sent to get them wouldn't be much good at tracking.

Dusk was settling when he spotted a cluster of buildings in the distance. He would have missed the fort but for the lanterns strung here and there—the only light for miles around. Mitchell blew out his cheeks with relief. He was about to slow the horses when he heard the telltale clip clop of horses approaching behind him. Hands still on the reins, Mitchell stood up and looked back. About five riders were closing fast. Mitchell yelled to speed the horses. The wagon swayed back and forth with the rough terrain. He realized there was no way he could reach the fort in time.

"Dang!" he muttered. "We got so close."

Mitchell looked all about, desperate. There had to be some way. He spotted the Winchester he had used on Pete earlier. Wrapping the reins around his arm, he lifted the gun and fired it into the air as many times as he could, whooping and yelling all the while. He thought his pursuers must surely be on him when he saw a troop of soldiers appear out of the front of the fort. It was only about one hundred yards away.

"Over here! I'm over here!"

Mitchell tossed down the rifle and found Earl's pistol, shooting off more rounds. As the pistol clicked empty, he realized he was surely a goner if this didn't work. A shot rang out from behind him. It sounded close. Answering shots from the soldiers in front filled him with equal measures of dread and hope. He was caught in the crossfire!

"Whoa!" he called to the horses, halting the wagon. Mitchell jumped off and rolled into the dirt. Bullets zipped back and forth. Mitchell kept his head low so he couldn't see what was happening. He fumbled at the chamber of the pistol he had kept in his hand as he jumped off the wagon. No bullets left. After a while, he heard the gunfire receding. He stood and looked about. In the gloom he made out the wagon had rolled a few yards forward. A rider was holding the reins, steadying the horses.

"Get away from that wagon," Mitchell said, making his voice threatening. "I've got my pistol here pointed at you."

Incredulous laughter erupted from the man on horseback.

"Mitchell Stone?" exclaimed Lieutenant Weed. "I should have known! Here was I thinking you wanted us to save you."

***

It was awkward getting the wagon to the fort in the dark. The horses were tired after being pushed so hard and unused to the rough terrain. Earl was conscious now and kept up a steady stream of chatter as they pulled in.

"Pretty well connected with that Lieutenant, ain't you? I reckon if you put a friendly word in for me, he won't give me much of a sentence. Those military have no interest in prosecuting people, anyway. Best thing might be for you to let me go. If you stop here, I'll just run off into the darkness. I'll never bother you again..."

Mitchell, sitting on the box-seat, half-distracted from trying to guide the tired horses, shook his head.

"You quiet down or I'll come back there and give you another tap."

Eventually, the wagon rolled past the fort's gates. In the poorly lit darkness, Mitchell could only make out a few soldiers and the outline of various artillery pieces.

"Mitchell," Weed called as his horse pulled up alongside. "You can put the wagon by the stables for the night."

"That's fine, Lieutenant," Mitchell replied. "What about them bandits? Did they give you much trouble?"

"No, no. They scampered as soon as we appeared. That was quick thinking to hide your tracks and come cross-country. Risky though..."

Mitchell shrugged.

"I had little choice. They'd have got me if I doubled back or kept on the trail. I got one of 'em tied up in the back of the wagon."

"That so?" Randolph said. "Pull up the wagon and let's look."

Mitchell got the wagon near the hitching post by the stables. Under a nearby lantern's light, the hostler took hold of the reins and looked to the tired horses. Mitchell jumped down and walked over to where the Lieutenant and another soldier were approaching the rear of the wagon.

"Time to come out, Earl," Mitchell said. "You don't want to make any more trouble for yourself."

Earl's head appeared behind the canvas.

"I can't," he said. "I'm trussed up like a hog!"

His service pistol pointed at Earl, Randolph motioned to a soldier. The soldier jumped in behind him and roughly tumbled the bandit out the back of the wagon.

"Oof!" Earl protested from the dirt. "You had no account to have done that. I would have come peaceably."

"As the representative for the United States Federal government," Randolph Weed said, voice hard. "I charge you with theft from, and murder of, members of the Pony Express. This could go badly for you as I can preside as a magistrate in your case."

"What? You don't understand! I never shot nobody. I was always just meant to be the driver. Listen, I know things. You heard of the Cochrane gang? Those boys forced me to do this—"

"Cochrane?" The Lieutenant's tone changed. "You know where he's hiding? How come he's got Paiute braves riding with him?"

Even sprawled on the ground wounded, Earl looked smug.

"I ain't sayin' nothin' tied up like this."

Randolph jerked his head at one of his men, who begrudgingly helped Earl up.

"Take him away. Put him in the brig for now. We'll see how much you really know in the morning."

"I know lots," said Earl over his shoulder as he's led away. "You'll see. Cochrane and his boys have got a big plan. Rilin' up the Paiute too…"

Lieutenant Weed shook his head.

"Ugh," he said to Mitchell. "Why did you save that scum?"

"I dunno. I'm not sure he tried to shoot anyone. I couldn't see from where I was hid in the back of the wagon, but… He's missing a trigger finger… Although, I'm sure he would have shot me if he could."

The Lieutenant sighed. Danger over fatigue and hunger overtook Mitchell. He sagged forward a bit.

"Goodness, Mitchell." Randolph said. "What you've been through! Come on into the mess hall and get some grub. You can give me the full story there."

The plain fare of the barracks was enough to revive Mitchell, to relate his latest adventures. Randolph listened with a bemused expression, interrupting with the occasional question.

"I don't like the sound of this 'John' that left you behind. Are you certain he was Paiute?"

"Hard to say for sure," Mitchell said, swigging back a cup of water. "He held back. Somethin' about the way he rode reminded me of them."

"That one you shot. I believe that's Pete Cochrane. His brother's the leader of the gang. I've never heard them allied with the Paiute before. They're the ones we're most worried about out here. Between them and the Comanche, the troops in the west are thinly stretched."

Randolph fell silent, mind occupied.

"Do you have enough men?" asked Mitchell.

Randolph looked up, making a face.

"That's the thing. The Union's been scrambling ever since Bull Run. Blasted Confederates are putting up more of a fight than anyone ever imagined. I wish I was back there myself, instead of being stuck out here scrambling after bandits and savages. But there it is."

Mitchell leaned back, considering his words. Although he was tired, he wouldn't rest easy unless he knew how things were settled.

"Yes," he agreed. "It might be worse back home, but here's bad enough. Pony Express can't operate with bandits attackin' 'em. Maybe I could get your men to come and visit my station every so often? Just an occasional patrol."

"Hmm. Yes. I suppose we could do that. Army uses the Pony Express for communications sometimes. I can justify it to my superiors."

"Can you give me an escort back to Egan Canyon? I reckon we've stirred things up with the local bandits and they'll be out for revenge."

"I'd like to, but it might be awkward," Randolph said, voice apologetic. "Can't spare any men immediately as we have to go after this Cochrane gang. We'll get the location of their hideout one way or another from our friend Earl."

"Maybe you can lend me a fast horse to get back with?" Mitchell asked, keeping the regret out of his voice. "You can pick it up when you come back to my station on patrol."

"Fair enough," Randolph said. "Why don't you have a couple of your men ready to return with us and pick up this wagon. I'm sure your company will want to get that back as soon as possible."

Mitchell nodded silently, mind occupied with the question of returning and relaying all this to Don in Salt Lake.

"Look at you!" exclaimed Randolph. "All business-like about your station. You're as bad as any General. Are you still certain you don't want to join us? You'd make a fine officer. I could put a word in for you."

"That's mighty kind of you, Randolph." Mitchell said with a bashful grin. "I made a promise to someone and I'm goin' to do what it takes to keep it.

Chapter Eight
Attacked by Paiute Warriors

The next day, Mitchell found Lieutenant Weed out in the yard readying his troops. They tied Earl to a light artillery piece behind a train of horses. He didn't look as pleased with himself as before.

"Earl will accompany us to the hideout," Weed said to Mitchell. "The Cochrane gang better be there, or we might just use him as target practice."

A soldier within earshot chuckled.

"I'll show you where it is," insisted Earl. "You'll see. Remember, I was only there because they kidnapped me. I'm an innocent bystander—"

"All right," Weed said, cutting him off. He walked over to Mitchell. "Sorry we can't accompany you to your station. Take whatever pony you want from the corral. I don't know how long this sortie is going to take, but you have my word that I will visit you as soon as I can."

"Thanks, Randolph. I truly appreciate that. I don't know about these military horses, though. They'd never do in the Pony Express."

"Beggars can't be choosers, my friend." Weed said with a laugh. "Good luck on your return."

"Best of luck to you and your men," Mitchell said. "That Cochrane bunch sounds pretty tough."

"Aw, what a touching scene!" Earl called. "I'm goin' to weep over here."

"Maybe I should have left you out there," Mitchell replied, shaking his head. "Goodbye Lieutenant."

Weed saluted Mitchell before turning towards Earl with a menacing look.

"It was just an innocent jest, Lieutenant," protested Earl. "I didn't mean nothin' by it."

Mitchell turned away with a chuckle and left them to it. He picked out the best pony he could find at the corral: a bay that was a little on the small side but looked the liveliest of the bunch. From the wagon, he found extra ammunition for his pistol. After all, he had been through, he didn't think he would ever again travel without some kind of firearm.

He retrieved the map and as much food as he could fit in his saddlebags. He even found a spare bugle, which he slung around his neck. As he made his last preparations, he watched Weed lead the bulk of his troops out of the fort. They towed several artillery pieces along with several troops on horses and on foot. It was going to be quite a show of force. Mitchell silently wished them well.

He mounted the bay and headed back on the trail. For a long while, he would turn and see the dust raised by the Fourth Artillery as they headed south. They surprised him at how slowly they travelled. Mitchell put the spurs to his horse and urged her forward.

"Welcome to the Pony Express!" he said to the animal. "You gotta be fast if you want to do well with this outfit."

The bay gave a surprised snort, shook her head, then galloped forward. Mitchell smiled. Maybe they would keep this one.

Mitchell found the return trip easy, and he made excellent progress. The weather wasn't too hot, and nobody was trying to shoot at him. Mitchell stopped at Simpson's Spring, the swing station before Egan Station. He had had to avoid it by taking the wagon cross-country. He explained to the astonished keeper what had happened to Stanley and Jim. The man cursed loudly and told Mitchell he had himself seen the Cochrane gang go thundering past one time. Mitchell warned him to be careful until the artillery had rooted them out.

Anxious to get back, Mitchell didn't tarry long. He set off, keeping the same speed as before. The sun was getting low when he arrived at the foothills. After a few miles, his horse made a frightened noise and reared into the air. Mitchell was nearly thrown from the horse.

"Whoa, girl!" he said, "What's got you riled?"

A pair of buzzards made an angry squawking sound and rose into the air before them. Mitchell suddenly realized where he was. Making calming sounds to the horse, he dismounted. The bodies were festering after being outside. He took out his canteen, took a quick swig and gave the rest to the horse. Stanley's body was the nearest. He could see Jim and Pete's back further. The carrion birds retreated to the further cadavers and were picking at them.

"Shoo! Get away from there!"

Mitchell waved furiously at the birds. They retreated sullenly to a nearby tree. Mitchell sighed heavily.

"I don't have a shovel to bury you, Stanley. Best I can do is try to cover you up with some rocks."

He couldn't make himself look at the faces as he pulled the bodies to a spot a small distance from the trail. They left tracks of blood, quickly absorbed in the dry soil. The smell was so bad, Mitchell had to cover his mouth with a bandanna. It took a lot longer than expected to find enough loose rocks to cover them.

Finally, he stood before the three mounds. The buzzards cawed loudly and flew off in disgust when they realized he would deprive them of their prize.

"Stanley, I'm right sorry to bury you beside the man that killed you. It's the best I can do right now. I'll make sure that someone comes back here with coffins for you both. I'm not much good at sayin' prayers, so I'll just be on my way."

With a sigh, Mitchell replaced his hat. He led the bay back on the trail. It was dark now, but he knew they couldn't be too far from the station. He mounted the horse and allowed her to trot slowly. The moon was rising full and helped their progress. A somber mood overtook Mitchell. Would he end up like that? Covered in rocks by the side of the road? He would be no use to Isabelle then.

"I don't care what Don says," Mitchell said aloud. "I don't think I can stick it out here for an entire year."

The horse blew out her lips in reply. Mitchell sighed. When they finally neared the station, he blew on the bugle to alert Frank. It made a mournful sound as it echoed off the lonely canyon walls.

"Mitchell?" Frank called, lantern aloft. "Is that you?"

"Evening, Frank. Have I got a story for you…"

"I'll bet! I was sure a rattlesnake or coyote got you. I went out tracking but couldn't find any trace. What the hell happened to you?"

"Looks like we got bandits and Paiute to contend with out here. They ambushed me."

"What!? Where did this happen?"

"'Bout ten miles down the trail. Three of 'em attacked the wagon. Killed Stanley and Jim."

Frank gave a low whistle.

"I was lucky," Mitchell continued. "I was hidin' out in the back of the wagon. Had to shoot one of 'em. Name of Pete Cochrane. Seems he's the brother of the leader of the gang. There was an older bandit by the name of Earl. I got him back to the fort. After we were chased by Paiute—"

"Hold on," interrupted Frank. "Fort? Paiute?"

"I got a lot to tell you," Mitchell said. "How 'bout we get this little bay settled for the night first."

Frank shooed Mitchell into the station while he tended to the animal, ensuring it was watered and fed properly. Wearily, Mitchell found some stale bread and cold beans to sustain himself. He did his best to answer Frank's questions when his partner returned, filling him in on the chase and the subsequent departure of Weed and his troops.

"Here's a thing," Frank said, after Mitchell lapsed into silence. "Like I said, I went traipsing around the hills yesterday looking for you. Come afternoon, I saw a rider across the canyon."

"A rider? What'd he look like?"

"Sun was behind him. Couldn't see him too clear. He stared at me a long time before galloping off. I don't know how long he had been watchin' me..."

"Think it was one of Cochrane's men? Or the Paiute?"

"I don't rightly know," Frank rubbed his stubbled chin. "He weren't friendly, that's for sure."

"I don't know about you," Mitchell said. "But I mean to keep my gun handy at all times. First thing tomorrow, I'm goin' to write a report to Don. One of us will have to bring it back to Salt Lake. If nothin' else, we'll need coffins for Stanley and Jim. They were employees of the Pony Express and Don will want to see them buried proper."

"You goin' to write a report?" Frank asked, cracking the slightest of smiles. "I thought you only wrote to your sweetheart back in Kansas."

"Never mind that," Mitchell replied with a wry chuckle. "How about I get you to write it? I am the one in charge after all."

"I'll write it," Frank said. "If you let me take it back to Salt Lake. Things are gettin' too hot around here for my likin'.'"

"I know what you mean," Mitchell agreed. "Too hot for me, too."

***

Mitchell woke the next day feeling oddly refreshed. It felt good having decided he would not stay out here too much longer. Once he got Frank to write the report, he would add a note to Don at the end to let him know of his decision. He shook off his slumber, dressed, and made his way to the outhouse. He mumbled his greetings to Frank, already up and making breakfast.

Mitchell stretched and squinted at the sun. It looked like the makings of a fine day. He frowned at a distant rumbling sound. Can't be thunder, he thought. The sky was too clear. *It couldn't be buffalo, could it?* Surely the enormous beasts wouldn't be interested in grazing the prickly bushes in here. Then he heard a distinctive whooping echoing off the canyon walls. Mitchell scrambled back inside.

"Frank!" he yelled. "Grab a rifle!"

"What?" said Frank. "I'm just—"

"Paiute!" Mitchell said, reaching for a Winchester. "Don't know how many, but they sure are makin' plenty of noise."

Frank dropped his griddle and took the rifle from Mitchell. Mitchell grabbed a second firearm, loading it with bullets. The racket from the Paiute braves was audible inside now. Frank peered out the window.

"Look at 'em come," Frank said. "What're we goin' to do, Mitchell?"

"Keep down!" Mitchell hissed. "They're liable to shoot through that window. Here. Help me with this."

Keeping low, Mitchell dragged their table to the door. Frank crouched beside to help.

"That ain't goin' to keep 'em out for long," Frank said.

"I know," Mitchell said. "But we don't have a lot of options."

They stayed as low as they could, listening to the braves gathering outside. The war cries stopped after a while. Silence descended, broken only by the occasional low whickering from a horse.

"We know you are in there," a voice called.

Mitchell's heart sank. He recognized that voice. Crawling over to the window, he snuck a glance outside. Standing Bear was at the head of the posse. He couldn't say for sure, but there were easily triple the number of Paiute braves from when they had taken him hostage. Mitchell ducked back down, sitting with his back against the wall.

"There must be near a hunnerd of 'em," he said.

Before Frank could reply, footsteps approached the door.

"Come out now and we will spare you," Running Bear said. He was just outside.

"Quick!" hissed Mitchell. "I'll hide the rifles. Now's our only chance."

There weren't many hiding places amongst the spartan furnishings of their station. Mitchell shoved them beneath the thin mattress of his bunk.

The wood of the door splintered, a tomahawk head appearing near the lock.

"All right! We'll come out! Just give us a minute."

Mitchell motioned to Frank to move the table again.

"But they'll kill us," Frank said in a fierce whisper. Mitchell shrugged.

"They spared me before. Let's just play along for now. We ain't goin' to win any shootout with that many outside."

They pulled back the table. At the sound, the hatchet stopped destroying the door.

"I'm opening the door now," Mitchell shouted. "We ain't armed."

Mitchell swung the door open. He raised his hands and stepped forward. Frank did the same, following close behind. Outside, the clearing around the station was dense with

Paiute warriors. Mitchell couldn't tell exactly how many, but it was easily over sixty. At the head of the throng, Standing Bear sat on a high black stallion. His eyes bulged with recognition of Mitchell.

"You!" he exclaimed. The shaman barked orders and the braves who were attacking the door grabbed him. Mitchell noted that Standing Bear's ceremonial outfit had changed. He looked more auspicious than before.

"Howdy," Mitchell said, trying not to wince as they pinned his hands behind his back.

"The Spirits are all powerful," exclaimed Standing Bear. "They have returned you to me to face retribution!"

"It's good to see you too," Mitchell quipped. "Looks like we've both come up in the world since we last met."

"Pah! Save your jokes," the shaman said. "I am leader now. We have new friends from other tribes that helped remove the old chief."

There was no mistaking the gloating tone to Standing Bear's words.

"Those friends include the Cochrane gang?" asked Mitchell. "The Spirits tell you to join up with them?"

Standing Bear gave him a malicious look. He spoke in Paiute to the braves behind him, gesturing at the corral alongside the station. A number dismounted, leading their horses into the enclosure. Standing Bear's nostrils flared as he visibly calmed himself before addressing Mitchell again.

"We showed you hospitality before," the shaman said. His smile was terrifying. "Now you return the favor. It is our way. My men are hungry. Some of them are starving. What can you offer us?"

"Does he want us to entertain him?" Frank asked, in a low whisper.

Mitchell shushed him.

"You did indeed show me great hospitality. I would like to do the same. Please come inside."

Mitchell half-turned toward the door. At least ten rifles cocked, and he halted. He was still being held by two braves. Standing Bear gave a quick nod, and they released Mitchell and Frank.

"Very good," said Standing Bear. "We accept your offer. Be careful. If we are not pleased, you will die."

"Certainly," said Mitchell. "Come on inside."

Mitchell was pretty sure they were fixing to murder them, anyway. This was just some ritual to justify doing so.

"C'mon," he whispered to Frank. "We gotta cook them something. Drag it out as long as you can."

Frank made a quick nod. They turned and headed back into the station. Standing Bear and his senior warriors poured in behind him. Mitchell noticed that several of them were looking around in amazement. This must be the first time they were inside a house.

"Why don't you gentlemen take a seat," Frank said, attempting a smile. They ignored him, curiously poking around the shelves and furniture. One found a revolver. He exclaimed and tucked it into his waistband. Standing Bear walked regally to the chair and took a seat. Two others joined him, sitting uncertainly.

"My men will take your guns, powder, and lead," he said matter-of-factly. "We will take your horses too. But first. Feed us!"

He pounded the table to accentuate his order. Both Frank and Mitchell jumped.

"Absolutely," Mitchell said. "Although if your braves keep taking the flour and salted pork, we won't have anything to feed you."

Standing Bear pursed his lips, then barked an order at the warriors raiding the supplies. The other men relented, putting down their plunder.

"All right, Frank," Mitchell said. "You're the cook here. What can we make these hungry savages?"

"I dunno," Frank replied. "Will they eat bread? I got some dough goin' in a bowl there."

"Does it take a while to put together?"

"Sure. I can stretch it out."

"Good. Gives me time to think."

There followed a surreal hour where Frank and Mitchell bent to making bread for their attackers. Some Paiute watched them with fascination. Others remained aloof, affecting disgust at these barbarous customs. Now and then, Standing Bear would announce some detail of the process in Paiute and English. Mitchell realized the shaman was showing off. He must want to impress them still, Mitchell thought.

"You must've been the star pupil back at the missionary," Mitchell couldn't help remark.

Standing Bear narrowed his eyes.

"We must learn from you," he barked. "In order to defeat you."

Mitchell shrugged and returned to baking.

Finally, they pulled a couple of loaves from the stove and laid them on the table before Standing Bear and his lieutenants. The warriors stared at the steaming bread. Inside the kitchen was sweltering from the hot day and having the stove stoked. The Paiute didn't seem to mind the sweaty interior.

"All right then," Frank said. "Go ahead."

Standing Bear gave a nod, and the men started ripping hunks of the bread, devouring them hungrily. Mitchell fidgeted while they consumed the food, wondering what to do next. A thought came to him.

"Why, you boys are right hungry!" he announced. "Why don't we make you some more."

Standing Bear paused his chewing to give Mitchell a suspicious look. He waited for a few moments, then nodded.

"I dunno," said Frank. "I might need more yeast..."

"Don't you worry. I'm sure there's some by the bunks. I'll just go get it."

One brave said something and Standing Bear replied. His voice had the same tone of explanation as before. Not waiting for permission, Mitchell ducked into their little room. He pulled out the rifle from under the bedding. The Paiute had raided here already but thankfully hadn't looked under the mattress. Mitchell wondered if it was because they weren't used to beds. He had to act quickly. He cocked the rifle and darted back to the main room. One brave spotted him and half-rose. Mitchell shot at the wall behind him.

"Everybody easy now!" he shouted. "Nobody move. Frank, go get your gun."

Standing Bear glared at Frank, who dashed back for his rifle.

"I should have known," the shaman said. "You will pay for this."

"I reckon you were going to make me pay, anyway," Mitchell replied, pointing the rifle at Standing Bear. "At least now we got a chance. Lunch's over. Frank, grab their weapons."

The braves relinquished their weapons with reluctance. One spat an accusation at Standing Bear, who blithely ignored them.

"All right," Mitchell said. "We're goin' to do this real slow. Anything goes wrong and you die first." He pointed the rifle at the glowering shaman.

"What do you mean to do?" Standing Bear asked. "My men have this place surrounded. They will hunt you down."

"I got you, don't I?" Mitchell replied. "An' you're their favored leader."

He motioned with his rifle for Standing Bear to rise. Mitchell went behind him, pointing the gun at his back. A quick conversation in Paiute followed, and the warriors exited, muttering.

"Tell them to get back from the horses. Go on!"

Standing Bear, seething with anger, cried out some more commands.

"All right, Frank. I guess we got to write that report now."

"What? We ain't got time for that."

"Just get some paper," Mitchell said, gun trained on the shaman. "Write 'Need Help at Egan Station'."

The braves had not touched the paper either. Frank quickly scribbled down the note. His hands were trembling as he did.

"All right. Let's put a *mochila* on that bay I brought back from Fort Laramie."

"Whatever for, Mitchell?"

"Don't worry. I got a plan. All right, Mr. Bear. Let's go outside."

Every warrior stared at them as Mitchell and Frank slowly led Standing Bear to the horse enclosure. Frank prepared the horse as quickly as he could, although he fumbled a few times. Mitchell motioned Frank back to him.

"All right," he whispered. "We only got one chance at this. Open that gate and shoo all the horses out."

There were about forty horses crammed into the little paddock. Frank opened the gate.

"Keep your rifle on Standing Bear here," Mitchell instructed. He went to the rear of the corral and fired his rifle twice. The frightened animals galloped out. Most of the Paiute warriors scrambled after their own horses.

"Sure hope this works," Mitchell muttered, watching his army horse escape southwards.

With a scream, a newly mounted brave shot at Mitchell. Mitchell ran towards the station, Frank alongside him. Standing Bear escaped. He yelled orders at his men. Gunshots rang out.

"Let's go back inside," Mitchell said. "We've a better chance—"

Mitchell watched in horror as Frank jerked backwards—his chest suddenly opened with a gaping hole.

"Frank!" Mitchell cried, turning towards his friend. He crouched over him. Frank's mouth was open, his eyes looked shocked. Mitchell didn't see the butt of the rifle that cracked down on the back of his head. He tumbled into blackness, onto his friend's body.

***

"Come on, Mitch," Isabelle murmured in his ear. "Let's see how fast we can go."

She was holding him close, both of them stuffed into the old mare's saddle. He laughed and urged the horse forward. Although only barely a man, he felt like the happiest man in the world. They cantered out along the dirt road. He knew they would have to return before sundown but, for now, they were free from drudgery and their disapproving parents. She laughed at the thrill of the wind rushing past, bringing a broad smile to Mitchell's face.

The memory of riding with Isabelle faded as they roused him by tossing a bucket of water over him. The water was foul, probably from the outhouse. He shook it out of his eyes, realizing his hands were tied behind his back. Vision blurred, he couldn't make out where he was, or why it was so dim.

"Where am I?" he called out. "Where's Frank?"

Standing Bear laughed. He was behind the brave who had woken Mitchell.

"Your friend? He is here beside you. Although I think soon he will join the Spirits. They will judge him then. As they will you. Soon."

"What?" Mitchell asked, panicked. "Frank? You alright?"

More laughter from Standing Bear, joined by the surrounding men. Mitchell's sight slowly cleared as he realized he was being kept in the tiny barn at the back of the station. He looked to his side. Frank was lying there: face pale, even in the dim light.

"Frank! Speak to me!"

Mitchell tried to tend to his friend, but his hands were tied. Mitchell gave a low moan, his breathing labored.

"Hah!" Standing Bear said. "You have nothing clever to say now?"

"You'll pay for this," Mitchell swore. "I'll see that you do."

"My men are preparing a pyre for you," Standing Bear said with a snort. "We will offer you to the Spirits to heal my people's hunger."

With that, the shaman swept from the little barn. His warriors followed, closing the door. Mitchell scrambled as close to Frank as he could.

"Frank! Can you hear me?"

"Water," croaked Frank. Mitchell gaped at the wound in Frank's chest. All he could see was a black mess in the dim light. The ground all about was slick with blood and foul water.

"Hey!" Mitchell yelled. "Can anyone hear me? He needs water!"

The Paiute guarding the door looked in.

"Water!" shouted Mitchell. "Can't you do something for this man?"

The jailor considered for a moment. He called out to another who returned with a pitcher. At least the water was from the well this time.

"Please, can you give it to him," Mitchell pleaded, showing his tied hands. "I can't help him."

The Paiute gave a shrug, then held the jug to Frank's mouth. Frank gasped and swallowed feebly.

"Mitchell? You there?"

"I'm here, Frank," Mitchell answered.

"I don't feel too good." Frank coughed painfully.

"You take it easy, Frank. We're goin' to get out of this."

"Sure," Frank said. "I feel awful cold though.."

The Paiute brave stood up and left them. Mitchell sat up and sidled over to Frank.

"Hey, you take it easy. I know we'll pull through this."

"That girl of yours," Frank asked. "What's her name?"

"Isabelle."

"You goin'…" Frank convulsed in painful coughing. It took him a while to recover. "You goin' back to her?"

"I am."

"You make sure…"

Frank groaned, unable to finish.

"Frank!"

The next sound was one Mitchell would never forget: the terrible rattle that emerged from Frank's throat. He called Frank's name several times but no reply came. Mitchell made such a commotion that the guard came in. He crouched over Frank's body, his hand over Frank's mouth.

"Dead," he said, without emotion.

Mitchell cried out in anger and frustration. The Paiute warrior gave him a look mixed of pity and contempt. He called out for more men. They dragged Frank's body from the barn. Mitchell yelled curses and impotent threats at them. Finally, they left him alone in the dark, bound and helpless.

***

The sun was low on the horizon when they dragged Mitchell out, wretched with despair. Two Paiute carried him by either arm. He looked ahead to where they had piled any wood they had found around a pole. They had already lashed Frank's body there. Standing Bear was dancing around the pile, a flaming torch in his hand. For once, Mitchell couldn't think of anything to say. He felt utterly defeated. Let them put me up on that pole, he thought, at least I'll join Frank.

Although he said nothing to Mitchell, there was a triumphant glint in Standing Bear's eyes as he performed his ritual. The warriors brought Mitchell to the pyre. They tied him there, his back facing Frank. Mitchell noticed they had smashed up most of the station's furniture to make the pile of wood for the fire. There was the little writing desk meant for reports. He had hoped to write to Isabelle on that, tell her he would not stay here much longer. He shook his head, blinking back tears. Standing Bear paused, a smug look on his face. He came right up to Mitchell's face.

"Now, you'll pay," he said. "For all your kind have done to my people."

He raised the torch, the flames were so hot Mitchell had to look away.

"The sun is setting now and you will join your friend."

Standing Bear stood back, waving the brand theatrically. He recommenced chanting, increasing the volume slowly. All the warriors gathered about, watching with little expression.

Mitchell looked away, screwing his eyes shut. Frank's body felt cold behind him.

The boom of a cannon echoed through the canyon.

Mitchell opened his eyes to see chaos all around. A surprised Standing Bear dropped the torch, and the wood started to ignite. In the firelight, Mitchell saw Paiute running about in confusion. From the south, he thought he heard horses and shouting. Some braves were shooting wildly in their direction.

"Help!" Mitchell yelled. "Can anyone help me!"

The flames were licking about his boots. Mitchell tugged at the rope pinning him against Frank. He couldn't move an inch. Another cannon shot boomed. An instant later, Mitchell watched in amazement as the ground nearby exploded in a shower of dirt, a couple of Paiute braves' bodies thrown in the air, landing like discarded dolls. Mitchell spotted the shaman, staggering about with his ceremonial garment awry. Men on horseback thundered in, shouting and shooting indiscriminately.

"Over here!" Mitchell cried. "I'm not goin' to last much longer."

He could feel his boots melting, flames rising all about. One rider halted his horse and did a double-take.

"Mitchell!" called Lieutenant Weed. "You men! Get him out of there!"

A couple of soldiers dismounted and rushed over. Many of the Paiute had retreated to the hills. They returned fire, but Weed's troops were well-armed, organized, and had the element of surprise. The soldiers pulled burning furniture back, kicking any flaming logs. Mitchell cried out as his toes burned. One soldier pulled a knife and cut Mitchell's bonds. Mitchell collapsed onto the hot ground and singed his cheek. They helped him up.

"Let's get you back to the station," a soldier said. "Ain't safe here. What about your partner?"

"Frank?" Mitchell said, panting from exertion. "He didn't make it."

They dashed for the building. Mitchell saw Standing Bear standing confused near the door.

"You demon!" cried the shaman. "What magic did you—"

They cut his words short as the soldier on Mitchell's left fired his revolver. Standing Bear jolted back, falling into the dirt.

At their leader's demise, the Paiute gave up any further resistance. Many found mounts and dissolved into the darkness, the rest ran off into the thicket. The soldiers lay Mitchell in his bunk and returned to make sure the fighting was over. Mitchell lay back, shocked he was still alive. He passed out for a few moments, overcome by events.

"Are you alright, Mitchell?" Weed asked, entering the room. "We have the area secured."

"Frank?" Mitchell asked, coming back to consciousness. "Did you save his body?"

"That your friend? Yes. We got him down before the fire did too much damage. Bad bloody business. Are you alright, though?"

Mitchell sat up. He felt at his feet. They were blistered but only superficially.

"I'll need new boots, I think."

Weed gave a wry chuckle.

"Was that your idea? To send our pony back?"

Mitchell could only nod in reply.

"You're lucky," Weed continued. "Taking the risk it would find its way back. We got the note. Truth be told, we had just returned from chasing down Cochrane. Otherwise, we wouldn't have come for another day or so. You're a lucky man, that was a close thing. What will you do now?"

Mitchell collapsed back in the bunk, overcome with relief. He sighed.

"I'm goin' home."

Epilogue

M itchell enjoyed opening the shop early. Few were around at this hour, and it often gave him time to tidy up. Sometimes he would take it easy and read from the latest copy of *The Wichita Eagle*. He looked over at the bundle of newspapers tied with string. *Might as well look...*

The little bell over the shop door dinged, distracting Mitchell from the paper. He looked up at the customer.

"Morning Mitchell," said Samuel Whittaker.

"Samuel," Mitchell said. "How can I help you?"

Mitchell tried to keep his voice neutral. They had had a time of it, keeping the bank from repossessing the store. Lucky thing Don Russell had given Mitchell a generous severance when he left the Pony Express. It meant they could hire an attorney to fight Fred Whittaker and his bank from trying to take possession of everything. Besides, something about Samuel Whittaker made Mitchell's skin crawl. They were grown men now, but Mitchell could recall some strange things from their childhood.

"Oh, I'm just passing the time of day," Samuel said, his voice bright.

"I got work to do," Mitchell said. "Don't have time to be wastin' chatting."

Isabelle sometimes scolded him about being too impatient with the customers. He was trying to improve, but he had no patience for a buzzard like Whittaker.

"Of course. Of course. It is important this store is run well. It belongs to my bank, after all."

"My attorney thinks different."

Mitchell struggled to keep his voice low. *Was Samuel threatening him first thing in the morning?*

"Oh, ho ho!" Samuel tittered. "No need to get so defensive. I'm sure we'll sort the whole thing out now that you're back. It must delight Isabelle to have you by her side."

Mitchell ground his teeth. Samuel Whittaker always unnerved him.

"We're gettin' married in a month. Now, either buy something or get out of my store."

"Your store?" Whittaker asked, eyebrow arched. "We'll see about that. Here's a writ from the sheriff giving you a day to vacate the premises." He placed an official envelope on the counter. "Take *that* to your attorney."

Mitchell looked at the letter, clenching his fists. His instinct was to jump over the counter and pound Samuel. Something about the unsettling smirk on his face made Mitchell realize that was just what he wanted. Mitchell took a deep breath. He missed being on the trail. If you faced a rattlesnake out there, you just shot it. Back home was different.

"You go to hell," he said to Samuel, calmly as he could.

Whittaker gave a disappointed snort.

"That's all you have to say? Not such a heroic cowboy now, are you? Good day."

Whittaker turned about and exited the store. The little bell dinged after him.

Mitchell blew out his cheeks in frustration and shook his head. He toyed with the envelope for a while, then tossed it aside. Reaching for the newspaper, he read the front page to distract himself. He quickly forgot his troubles as he read in amazement:

PONY EXPRESS TO CEASE OPERATION

Salt Lake City,Utah October 28, 1861

After a little over a year in operation, the Central Overland Pony Express announced they are shutting down operations. Citing the high cost of running a dangerous business and the recent completion of the transcontinental telegraph, the owners Russell, Majors, and Waddell made the regretful announcement today...

The End

Thanks for taking the time to read this story. A positive review on Amazon would be appreciated.

Made in the USA
Monee, IL
06 June 2022